THE SPACE MEN

THE JOHN KIRK OF ARES SERIES

The Winged Men

The Invisible Men

The Space Men

Other Books by Gary Lovisi:

Driving Hell's Highway

Gargoyle Nights: A Collection of Horror

Mars Needs Books!: A Science Fiction Novel

Murder of a Bookman: A Bentley Hollow Collectibles Mystery Novel

Violence Is the Only Solution

As Editor:

Battling Boxing Stories

The Great Detective: His Further Adventures:
A Sherlock Holmes Anthology

THE SPACE MEN

The Jon Kirk of Ares Chronicles: Book 3

GARY LOVISI

Map of Ares by Lucille Cali

*A Scientific Romance inspired by Edgar Rice Burroughs'
John Carter Series and set upon the faraway planet Ares*

WILDSIDE PRESS

NAMES OF PEOPLE AND PLACES APPEARING IN THE JON KIRK CHRONICLES

ALUN KIRK: the son of Emperor Jon Kirk and Lady Sirah of the Green Empire of Ares. At this time he is still a baby boy but he will become as great a warrior as his father.

ANCIENT BOOK OF KOR: a mythical lost tome said to possess the super-science of the ancient people of Ares.

ARON THE ELDEST: elder and mind-power master of the Old Ones of Keva.

AR-DEN: ancient wise man and one of Jon Kirk's most important counselors.

BLACK DRAGONS, THE: mounted riders and warriors who are the body guard of Emperor Jon Kirk.

BLUE KORTAS: alien blue-skinned horned mercenaries, large mutant well armed killers not native to Ares and brought in to fight for The Secret Empire.

BRAN: one of The Secret Empire prisoners and a pirate from the planet of Ko-Ah-Leh who befriends Jon Kirk.

CALIAT: one of the six green cities on the continent of Cos on the planet Ares occupied by the Zaran Winged-men and then set free by Jon Kirk and Tar-gool, renamed Tarcos in honor of Tar-gool.

CAVES OF CONSCIENCE: a huge network of caves north of Tarcos in the Coastal Mountains that Jon Kirk used as his headquarters during the invasion of Ares.

CONSIGNATS: impressed fighters, or slaves, forced to fight for The Secret Empire of The Hundred Worlds.

DARK NIGHT: Flagship of Lord Protector Doom leader of The Secret Empire fleet in orbit around Ares.

GENERAL ZOD: military leader of all Blue Korta empire shock troops.

GORM: of the Gorms, a large Viking-sized alien who befriends Jon Kirk.

HE WHO IS NOT TO BE NAMED: also known by the words Kin-Ty-Roo, said to be Emperor of the Known Universe and master of what is called The Enemy Empire, which is locked in a vicious war with The Secret Empire of The Hundred Worlds ruled by the Sindaki Lords.

HUNDRED WORLDERS: short name for minions of The Secret Empire of the Hundred Worlds, also known as The Secret Empire, ruled by the Sindaki Lords.

JON KIRK: Emperor of The Green Empire of The Six Cities of Ares and Earthman hero, husband to Empress Sirah, father of Alun Kirk.

KAL-SAR: Imperial governor of one of the Six Cities who defied Jon Kirk's order to evacuate his city and fought the Blue Kortas. His entire army and civilian population was massacred by the enemy.

KEV: hidden city on the western continent of Ares. See Keva.

KEVA: ancient hidden city of the Greens whose people have great mind powers, destroyed by a ship of Lord Mentep's fleet and later rebuilt and renamed Kev in a secret location on the western continent of Ares.

KIN-TY-ROO: words to indicate the being called Emperor of the Known Universe, the words roughly translate into the phrase "He Who Is Not To be Named", but this being is a complete mystery but is master of what is called The Enemy Empire.

LARL: Mythical ancient Ares youth, son to hero Ry-Nar who entered the body of the dread Zarbane monster to retrieve his body.

LORD PROTECTOR KARLATH DOOM: Lord Protector and leader of the Secret Empire of the Hundred Worlds fleet in orbit around Ares. His flagship was *Dark Night*. Doom is a Sindaki, a race who is said to have unnatural mystical powers.

MANALIA: wife to Zaor, Jon Kirk's most trusted friend and general of the Green Empire army of Ares.

NEWCOMERS: general name of the minions of The Enemy Empire troops under the Kin-Ty-Roo or Emperor of The Known Universe.

POLN: female *felina* tiger creature who befriends Jon Kirk.

QUARTO: Winged-man from Zar who is the captain of *Dark Night*, the flagship of Lord Protector Doom of The Secret Empire of the Hundred Worlds, later becomes Admiral Quarto-Zar of the fleet.

RAS-NOOR: Ares scientist, associate of the great Tar-gool, master scientist of Ares and the man whose machine brought Jon Kirk from Earth to Ares.

RY-NAR: Ancient Ares warrior hero who entered the dread monster Zarbane to retrieve the body of his son Larl, much in the manner of Jonah and the whale on Earth.

SAHN-JOR: friend of Jon Kirk and the First Minister and administrator of the Green Empire of Ares.

SECRET EMPIRE, THE: known as The Secret Empire of The Hundred Worlds, interplanetary empire of which the Winged-men from Zar are a part, a very small part, and which is seeking to reestablish Zaran rule on Ares and enslave the greens-skinned humans and destroy Jon Kirk and his Green Empire.

SHAMAR: young king of the mind-powerful people of Keva, later he is king of Kev, and a friend to Jon Kirk.

SHARN: Leader of the alien Tergats and sub-commander who runs the control room of the prison ship *Solar Happiness*, and who joined with Jon Kirk.

SASHEEN: merman from the sea world of Talu who befriended Jon Kirk.

SHORNS: a religious sect on Zar whose Winged-men adherents believe in peace and non-violence. They do not eat meat or people. Captain Quarto is a Shorns.

SIRAH: Empress of The Green Empire of Ares and wife to Earthman and Emperor Jon Kirk. Mother of Alun Kirk.

SLOSS: Ares word for garbage, or lies.

SOLAR HAPPINESS: prison ship of the Secret Empire captured by Jon Kirk and his companions.

TAMBU: a Gorm from the planet Gorm who is a blood brother and companion to the huge Viking-like alien creature called Gorm.

TAR-GOOL: an old man, master scientist and patriot of the green-skinned humans of Ares, friend of Jon Kirk. He was killed in the battle to free the city of Caliat from the Zaran Winged-men, the city of Caliat was renamed Tarcos in his honor.

TERGATS: race of tall, gangly yellow-skin humanoids with fins under control of the Secret Empire. Sharn is a leader of the Tergats.

TOR-NUL: Captain of Emperor Jon Kirk's imperial bodyguard, the Black Dragons.

WINGED-MEN: the brutal flying creatures from the planet Zar who have terrorized, murdered and eaten the green-skinned humans of Ares for millennia, also called Zarans.

ZAOR: Jon Kirk's most trusted captain and best friend on the planet Ares, brother of his wife, Sirah. General of the Green Empire army.

ZAR: home world of the Winged-men, one of the planets in the Orion star system.

ZARBANE: a mythical massive vicious monster of ancient Ares texts. Heroic Ry-Nar entered such a beast to retrieve his son Larl's body.

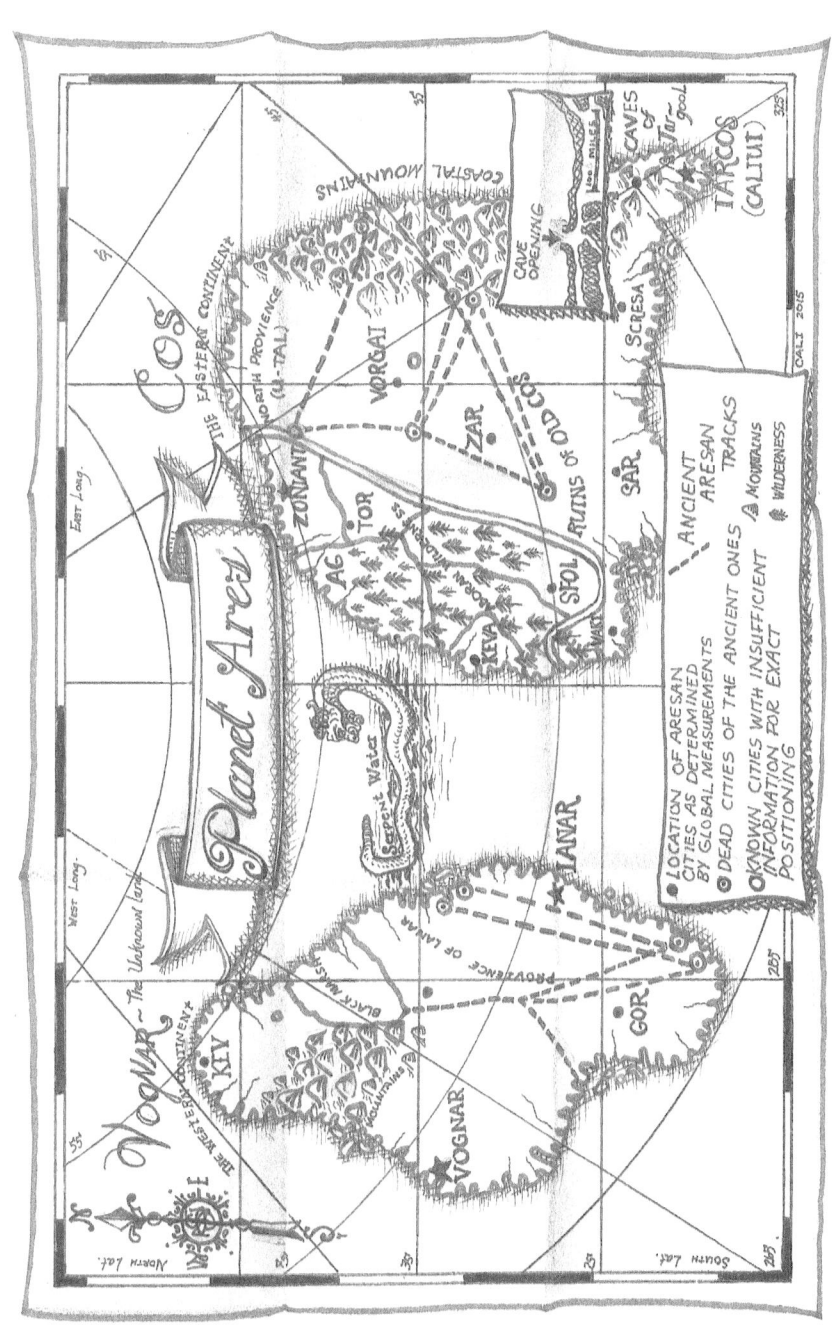

CHAPTER 1

JON KIRK RETURNS!

Many years had passed. I was getting on with my life. I had married my college sweetheart Margaret, and was raising our three children into their teen years. I had all but forgotten about my long-ago friend Jon Kirk and his wonderful adventures upon the mysterious and faraway planet of Ares.

And while I had received a second manuscript chronicling more adventures of my good friend, that had been a long time ago, and I had heard no word of him since then. Time slipped away over the years and eventually events on Ares became dusty memories in my life. I grew older, was married, had children, life went on for me. I had not heard from Jon Kirk for some years. So time passed and I moved on. Eventually I forgot all about Jon Kirk.

But it seems that Jon Kirk did not forget about me!

As suddenly as Jon Kirk had disappeared from my life, he reappeared in my life one day not long ago.

Margaret had taken the kids away for the week to visit her mother with a sleepover in the next town. As I was a writer with a tight deadline, I had stayed home alone to finish that important project. I had just turned off the computer and was ready to make a pot of coffee and attack a box of donuts when suddenly the doorbell rang.

"Now who can that be at this hour?" I wondered aloud. I was alone and expecting no one.

I ran downstairs, fumbled with the latch of the front door, and upon opening it, saw a man framed in the doorway whose image came to me out of the dark recesses of my memory. He was tall, lean, with the well-muscled physique and well-toned body of the fighting man. He had pitch black hair, close-cropped, and steel-grey eyes that shone with bold intelligence. And there was a broad winning smile upon his face. He did not appear to have aged a day since I last saw him many years ago. It was astounding! Of course I recognized him right away, but I was so shocked and surprised by his presence here I could barely believe what my eyes showed me.

"Jon?" I stammered incredulously. "Jon Kirk? Is it really you?"

He laughed at my sudden surprise with that good-natured sense of humor he was well known for and said simply, "Hello, old friend, yes it is I. It has been a while."

"I… I…" Well, I hardly knew what to make of this or what to say in response.

Jon Kirk smiled warmly, patient with me as always.

"How can you be here?" I blurted unable to hold back my surprise.

My friend gave me a warm grin, "I did tell you about Tar-gool and his space travel machine on my last visit to you. Do you not remember?"

"Oh, yes, of course" I recalled, feeling rather foolish. Tar-gool had a machine that could transmit Jon Kirk's voice and image across the vastness of space as if he were actually here with me now. It was amazing. Obviously that machine was in use now and that is how I was able to communicate with my friend and see his image before me.

"Well, aren't you going to invite me in?" my visitor asked with a wry grin.

I startled, shook my head to clear the cobwebs, "Yes, of course. Oh, Jon, it's so good to see you! By all means, come in, please sit down. Well, how are you? How is Sirah? What? Where? I… I have a million questions!"

Jon just laughed in that hearty booming voice of his, "Easy, my friend, all in good time. We have all night. I have a lot to tell you and I know you are full of questions…"

"Questions! Jon, you have no idea! It's been years! What has happened?"

Jon Kirk smiled, sat down, got comfortable, then asked, "Well, where should I begin?"

"Begin! Why, at the beginning, of course! Let me see, if I remember correctly, Tarcos was under siege when last I read of your adventures in that manuscript you had sent to me. You had won a furious battle, the Grand Fleet of Lord Mentep of the Blues was attacking and had been defeated by the mind powers of the mysterious Kevans. What happened next? Did you attack Zar? I also recall a child was on the way," I blurted out, remembering where he had left off in that second narrative of his adventures he had sent to me so long ago.

"Yes, Sirah and I now have a son, Alun Kirk, a strong boy, he takes after us both in many ways," Jon Kirk replied with pride, then he allowed a little grin. "He is rather a handful."

I smiled, "A son! That is great, Jon, I am so happy for you both, but what of everything else?"

"Yes, that was all a long time ago, a lot has changed, so many incredible adventures, war, revolution, the fight for freedom of my adopted world the planet Ares, freedom from the dread Winged-men of Zar. And then there was the space war—with the Secret Empire—and so much more!"

I had never heard mention of that last part by him before and I repeated that ominous phrase, "The Secret Empire? Jon, what is that? Can you tell me about it?"

"Yes, my friend, I will tell you all about it. It is a dark, vile and alien story of a secret interplanetary empire. Empires, in fact! There are *two* of them, you see. Well, to begin with it appears that this Secret Empire were, in fact, the prime movers behind the Zaran Winged-men who had conquered and occupied the human world of Ares thousands of years previously. They are an empire made up of over a hundred space-faring races who are our enemies. They have ruled many worlds, and upon Ares they have helped to keep the green-skinned humans as slaves, and worse, for more than a thousand years."

"You must tell me everything!" I blurted as I starred at my friend wide-eyed, astonished that he was actually right there before me. I was so excited to hear his latest wild tale I could not speak.

"First, let me give you some background, my friend, and thereby bring you up to speed on my incredible story."

I nodded enthusiastically. I sat down across from him all eagerness as I prepared to be whisked away to a strange planet of wonder and adventure—Jon Kirk's world—the mysterious planet Ares!

* * * *

"I have already told you the story of the war for Aresan freedom against the Zaran Winged-men. That was a hearty struggle, let me tell you. But suffice it to say, for the limits of this narrative," Jon Kirk told me softly, "that with my allies, I was eventually able to conquer the five remaining Zaran Winged-men cities on Ares. We were able to free the green people of Ares, or at least those upon the eastern continent of Cos. Those enemies we did not kill, we routed—those who did not run, died. In two years time the power of the Winged-men was crushed upon Ares and their six cities were re-conquered and back under control of the Greens—the humans of Ares.

"Next we defeated the Blues—or the blue-skinned Vognars and their Supreme Leader the brutal tyrant, Okvon. His Grand Fleet under Lord Admiral Mentep was utterly destroyed. Here the Kevans helped us with their mind powers. Our victory was a great time of joy and happiness for the people of Ares and the many friends I have made upon my adopted world.

"Well, after all that war we had a brief respite which that victory brought to us, it was a time of great calm and it was wonderful. That was when Sirah gave birth, and my son, Alun, was born. It was the happiest day of my life. Alun Kirk. He is a prince of the Green Empire they say, but to me and his mother he is just a lovely little boy. So life was good. It certainly appeared our enemies were on the run. We only learned later that a small group of the Winged-men had somehow escaped us by going off-planet. I assumed they were going to get help from Zar, but we heard nothing more about them for some time."

"Off-planet? So the rumors you told me last time about the Winged-men being decedents of conquerors from some other world were true, Jon?"

"Yes, they have come from the world of Zar, another planet in the Orion system. Near Ares. But there is more, my friend. Much more. A mass of tangled and sinister alliances and devious machinations, and behind it all a Secret Empire that controls all the planets of The Hundred Worlds. They control Zar, which was only one of those hundred worlds, and Zar had controlled Ares, and now that space empire had sent a battle fleet to re-conquer and occupy Ares and place it firmly under the control of the Zaran Winged-men once again. It was a war begun to enslave my adopted people, the green people I love and respect who had only recently tasted the sweet flavor of freedom—a new war begun to enslave them for thousands of years more. I would not allow that to happen.

"Of course not!" I shouted in excitement, then I calmed down and asked, "What did you do about it, Jon?"

Jon Kirk smiled a bit at my over exuberant enthusiasm, then sighed, remembering, as memories flooded into his mind, and he looked at me and spoke softly, "My friend, I prepared for war and I made sure we would win! What I did was gather our hosts together and prepare to fight whenever and wherever the enemy ships landed. Our scientists at Tarcos determined from various high-ranking Zaran prisoners, that there was a Secret Empire of The Hundred Worlds space fleet making their way to Ares. But before I was able to form the defensive and offensive tactics to engage this new enemy, my true old enemies, treachery and betrayal reared their ugly head and they engaged me with disastrous results!"

I nodded, open-mouthed, enthusiastic to hear more. Whatever did he mean? I looked at his stern face closely and waited patiently for him to tell his story.

Jon Kirk sighed broadly, then continued, "I always look to the sky, my friend. When you look up into the sky, it is there where you will see the most amazing things, and sometimes even, the warships of your enemy approaching."

CHAPTER 2

THE SECRET FLEET

The blood red sun of Ares raced across the crimson sky like an angry messenger of war as night soon settled over my new world of turmoil and death once again.

Having reluctantly been proclaimed emperor of the new Green Empire of Ares, I was responsible and concerned for the future of my people—the people I had helped to free and the people I now must lead. I also had a wife and son now, so my roots were firmly planted in Ares soil. I was concerned with the fate of my new world as if it were my own home world of Earth. Perhaps even more so. I wanted to ensure that my brave people did not loose the freedom they had fought so hard to win in the days and years ahead. I knew I had cause for concern.

The Zarans, the bestial Winged-men of Zar who had so recently been masters of our world, were a devious and relentless lot. I knew they would never give up or seek a peaceful settlement to our conflict, even though I tried to do so with them many times. Their breaking of all treaties was bad enough and expected. However, when your peace ambassador's head is sent back to you separate from his body in answer to your plea for negotiations, you do not need the meaning of that answer written out in words for you to see clearly just where things stand. Nevertheless, I still held out hope for peace between the two races, even as those Winged-men that remain alive after the defeats of Grusus and Bron, had gone off into the mountains to hide and regroup their forces. I knew they had another leader now, much as Bron had promised me they would when I had fought him to the death, so I knew that another attack was coming.

Sahn Jor and Zaor, my ablest minister and general, and my best friends since I had first come to their world so long ago, agreed with me and kept their troops in a state of heightened readiness. The governors of each of the six newly liberated cities—each one a trusted agent appointed by myself and our new governing council in reward for their valor and dedication to Ares freedom—did all they could to ready their cities for attack and siege. They built up their fighting forces with levies from the surrounding countryside and enhanced training of male and female troops.

As emperor of the Six Cities of the Green Empire—mostly all of the green-skinned people of Ares—I did my best to coordinate our defense from my capital city of Tarcos. Yet I was disturbed the way events were progressing. I felt an ominous presence, a feeling that the very planet itself was under some kind of force or mysterious dark influence. Something was brewing and it was bad. I know it seems incredible but I know what I felt and when I questioned others such as my beloved wife and Empress, Sirah, as well as friends, warriors and nobles at court, I received the same answer. Everyone felt an inexplicable dark presence or force hanging over us like a sinister veil. A feeling of doom seemed to be hanging over us. What convinced me though, was when our most talented scientist, Ras-noor, a disciple of the great Tar-gool, reported that his instruments showed that the planet was indeed being bathed in a mysterious space ray of some kind.

"Is it lethal, or dangerous?" I asked Ras-noor in alarm, for his words had me very concerned and I knew that such a powerful light source must only have dire consequences.

"No, Jon Kirk, it does not seem so, not in the general sense," Ras-noor replied, much to my surprise. He was an older man, a master scientist and a long-time Ares patriot who had fought well against the Winged-men in our fight for freedom. He had helped us fight the Blue Vognars and had been well trained by the Old Ones of Keva, including Aron The Eldest.

I nodded, and looked at him carefully, afraid to hear of the unspoken fear I knew he felt. "So, what do you mean exactly?"

"Well, that my emperor, is what is so strange to me. The space ray has but little effect upon me or anyone else I can discern, it does not seem to be dangerous, but it is noticeable, measurable. There is something definitely there, bathing our world from off-planet, from out in space. It may be a natural phenomenon, from the red Ares sun, but it may not. I think not. It is certainly new and strange, foreign to our world for certain. I believe that it may be a space beacon of some kind."

"A space beacon? How is that possible?" I demanded, wondering just what that could mean now.

"That is the question, My Lord," Ras-noor replied with a dark look, "but it surely is some type of beam bathing our world. And, it may be something more, perhaps worse."

"A space beacon is bad enough. What could be worse?" I demanded, feeling a tightness now grow in my gut at this dire news.

"I am sorry, I am not sure, My Lord."

"Well, find out, Ras-noor. Find out!"

"Yes, My Lord!" the aged Ares scientist nodded, bowed, then left the room to set to work on finding me some answers. I wondered exactly what he would find out and what it would mean for my people and for Ares. A ray from space bathing my world in a beam of what? Where was it coming from? Who was responsible? And what was it doing to my world? I did not sleep well that night as I awaited Ras-noor's report.

The next day the aged scientist attended me in the grand palace audience chamber and made his report. Well of course Ras-noor soon hit upon the correct answer. The space ray was indeed a homing beacon, and it was deployed for an armada of space vessels coming to Ares from what was known as the Secret Empire of The Hundred Worlds. No one had ever heard of this empire, but it was a vast space-faring empire, and the realization of what that meant filled me with dread. At the time I was sure they were from Zar, the home of the Winged-men, on their way to attack Ares with the aim of enslaving all the Greens once again. Well, as far as I was concerned, that would not happen while I lived!

I ordered Ras-noor and his staff to continue with their research and get me answers on this space beacon and what it meant.

I knew I had to act swiftly for I felt an attack was imminent. I organized the city watches and rebuilt the army. I strengthened the fortifications of the cities to make sure they were safe. Then I knew I had to go on the offensive. We still had some of the Vognar airships. We also had the device that created invisibility and my scientists knew how to harness the forces of the white beam projector. The Kevans had helped us with these weapons in those last days before they left us to hide, secreting themselves away from all men. It was their way. However, even without the Kevans we now had super weapons we could use that would help us fight—and even win against any invading force from Zar.

Or so I thought at the time. As it turned out, things would become a lot more complicated.

CHAPTER 3

BLUE KORTAS

The first intruder ship was tracked when it landed on the Shiva Plains near the River Afar. My army was now ready, ten thousand of the best trained Ares warriors, made up of both Greens and Blues, led by myself, Zaor, Sahn Jor, and many of the heroes of the fight for freedom on Ares.

Riding upon the back of our swift Ares horse-like beasts, our cavalry struck fast with a mad charge across the plain to intercept the first enemy space vessel as it landed. Strangely enough, this was the first and only enemy vessel to land in the area, even though our own sensors and enhanced vision devices told us that there were more than one-hundred ships now in orbit around our world. If so, why did only one ship land upon our soil? I could venture a guess based on strategy, but I did not want to consider that dark possibility—that that was all our enemy needed to achieve their purpose. I held out hope that their reason for landing was to negotiate, or perhaps set up some preliminary camp. If the later was the reason, we would take them out quickly here and now. Others had their own thoughts on the mystery and voiced them to me.

"It seems obvious, Jon Kirk," Zaor told me with hopefulness in his eyes. "The enemy are here to sue for peace, or at least to make some kind of deal with you."

I shrugged, not at all convinced.

With a shake of his head Sahn Jor added, "More likely, they want to talk, but only to give us some kind of ultimatum. Or to set up some kind of base camp for their invasion of Ares."

I nodded, "Now that seems a bit more realistic."

Little did I know that neither of those two quite logical possibilities were the reason why that lone and mysterious enemy space vessel had landed on Ares. In fact, the truth behind this alien landing was much more sinister and dangerous than any of us could ever have surmised at the time.

I sensed something here was not right. I told Zaor, "Hold back your column. And Sahn Jor, I want your group to hold back also and set up a defensive perimeter along that ridge. I'm going forward by myself with just one company of my Black Dragons, a few imperial bodyguard should be more than enough to protect me from any enemy mischief. We can still use the invisibility device if need be to shield us from their eyes."

Zaor and Sahn Jor were not at all happy by this lone move on my part and protested strongly, but I would have none of it. I was the leader of these people, I would go forward as a leader with pride and do my duty.

Since the war with the Blues, we had taken their secret weapons and now had use of them for the Green Empire and my warriors. The most important of these were the powerful beam projectors, but just as important was the invisibility device—which I had mass-produced and issued to each of our warriors. It was a wonderful weapon, but one not without some setbacks—for while it made the wearer invisible—once invisible warriors could not see each other either. So it had to be used judiciously. There were complications with warriors going to invisibility that still needed to be worked out. I had no doubt we could correct these problems eventually, but it would take time—time we did not have now. But if worse came to worse, I would launch our attack against these intruders with an entirely invisible army that no invaders would be able to see—and never be able to stand up against.

However, as my small force got ready to move into position nearer the invaders ship this entire situation gave me pause for great concern. As the old expression went—I smelled something rotten in Denmark. Something was not quite right here. I felt it may be a trap, or maybe even something worse.

Before I proceeded forward I called Zaor to my side, "Good friend and brother, I want you to take your force of warriors and ride back to Tarcos. Protect Sirah, and your beloved Manalia, and begin the evacuation of the city. Order the governors of the other five cities to do likewise. Make it orderly, but make it fast, we have no time to lose, if what I believe is going to happen will happen. We must make sure we evacuate all the cities!"

Zaor looked at me aghast, shaking his head, "But, Jon Kirk…?"

I gestured for him to be quiet and obey. Zaor was the bravest of the brave, a warrior to whom anything but head-on battle was against his heroic nature. But this was a different situation and I looked at him sternly, for I knew what we were up against here now, something none of the people of Ares had ever seen before in their long lives. True, we had a few Vognar airships, a few beam weapons, and the invisibility device, but I knew that now we were not going up against any Ares enemy now, but a technologically advanced space-faring alien enemy. That made a big difference. They would be a more advanced space-faring race. They would have all our weapons—and more!

"No, Zaor, our cities and their walls are no match for what is coming, high walls will not offer our people protection against this fleet or their weapons. Our people in the cities will be sitting ducks for slaughter. Now be off! I order it!"

Zaor nodded, he did not understand my term "sitting ducks' but he surely understood the word slaughter and what that meant. Then his face grew hard.

"We should attack now, with all our forces, make the entire army invisible, with that power no one can stand against us!" he said hopefully, pleading.

"No," I insisted. "Please listen to me, and heed my orders, my friend."

Zaor shook his head, then nodded, "Of course, My Emperor."

When Zaor and his force of five thousand had ridden off, and Sahn Jor's force of five thousand, the remaining half of my army now dismounted and set up a hard defensive perimeter. Then I rode down across the Shiva Plain with my small group of Black Dragons, a detachment of my personal imperial bodyguard, to investigate this enemy ship from space that had now landed upon Ares. I needed to view them up close.

Immediately I told my men to go to full invisibility, switching on our personal invisibility devices—the small box-like device that was attached to each of our belts. It was then that we had our first great shock.

I looked to my lieutenant, Par-took, "You and your men have forgotten to switch on your invisibility devices. Do so now."

"They are on, My Lord. They do not seem to work," Par-took replied fumbling with his device and the switch.

I checked my own device as did each of the men with me. The devices were clearly not functioning. Not one of them was working, so I was sure it could not be some kind of mechanical error. Now we had no invisibility. I was alarmed at this realization, because this changed everything.

Then my mind recalled the talk I had had with Ras-noor about the strange space ray that he thought might be some type of beacon directing the invading space fleet to Ares. He had also mentioned to me that he thought that it might have some other purpose, but could not tell me what that might be at the time. Now I knew that it was a beam that somehow was jamming our invisibility devices. I told this to my men and they were not happy by the news, but not one wavered in his resolve to follow me. Now we had no trump card in our scouting mission—nor could I order a full-on attack later. That attack was out of the question now. However, I still needed to go forward and discover what this enemy was and what they had in mind. So I must check this landing party and see what I could learn about these intruders.

When we reached a small ridge above the alien ship I saw it was an incredibly massive space vessel and that it was already open and spewing forth hundreds of the strangest warriors I had ever seen. I was surprised by the look of them. These beings were not Winged-men at all, but something very different and it would turn out, far worse. They reminded me of some kind of Nazi German SS shock troops from my memories of them way back in Earth history books and films. They were unlike any Ares people I had ever seen and could not be from Ares at all. That was important. They were out-worlders, like me. They were not armed with swords either, but held large projectile firing weapons. They all carried guns! *Guns on Ares!*

I would later learn that these creatures were Blue Kortas, deadly vicious mercenaries from a brutal blue world far away. They were huge blue mutant beasts bred for war and fighting. At first I thought they wore what appeared to be old-time Viking horned war helms, but when I saw them closer, I could see that the creatures indeed had horns that protruded from the sides of their heads. Their helmets had two holes in the sides that allowed the white pointed horns to protrude through. It was quite effective and terrifying. They rode upon the back of special mounts they had brought with them called *phars*, huge three-legged birdlike beasts that did not fly but had long two-pronged dragon-like tails and were formidable fighters themselves. A *phar* with a Blue Korta upon its back made a deadly team and a most intimidating threat. No Ares warrior could stand up against them or their weapons. My heart sank.

And of course now, our forces could not use the power of invisibility! That had been my trump card in any reconnoiter or attack, now that was useless.

These Blue Kortas were all well armed with what I would learn soon were laser spears and projectile rifles! It was incredible. My heart sank as the full realization of what had come to my adopted world lay clearly before me. My people could never fight these creatures and win, and the realization just broke my heart. We were already beaten. It was not pessimism, it was sound military reality based upon tactics and strategy. We were severely outmatched. If I ordered an attack it would become a massacre.

I watched with awe as the huge ship spewed out hundreds, and then thousands, of these invaders in well regimented armed groups. They appeared very well organized. I looked at this new enemy more closely with trepidation. They were each heavily armed. Each Blue Korta wore bandoleers of explosive bullets and grenades and they seemed to be wearing some type of body armor. They wore helmeted headdresses with mask-like faces and bright colored feather-like plumage. They were at once gruesome, terrible, barbaric and glorious to behold. But more than anything I knew about them, they were deadly to my warriors and the people of the Six Cities of Ares who would be no match for them or their more advanced projectile weapons. My fledgling Green Empire was in serious trouble. Without being able to use our invisibility devices we were doomed and now I knew I would have to begin a serious change of strategy and tactics. It would be a change my warriors and the Greens would not like at all—but it might just save them from mass extinction.

I looked upon rank upon rank of orderly enemy troops lined up and ready for action and I could only sigh with a grim desperation and an icy chill of deadly doom that grasped my insides and would not let go of me. What could I do? How could I protect my people? They had installed me as their emperor—much against my wishes—but I had reluctantly accepted that responsibility. Now the duty had fallen to me to protect them. Now what was I to do? Was I to battle against this force using my heroic sword-wielding warriors—as brave as they were? I knew it would prove hopeless. It would become a mass slaughter. We no longer had the use of invisibility. The battle would be our swords against their guns. I shook my head sadly. It was a bitter pill to swallow.

My thoughts flashed back to Earth history in 1939 and the glorious Polish cavalry lancers. The Polish Calvary was known as the best cavalry in the world at that time—but they were torn to pieces when they went up against Hitler's German Panzer tanks with canons and machine guns. It had been an incredibly brave attack, even glorious by some standards, but it became horribly useless slaughter. Such a stupid waste of brave soldiers. I did not want to repeat that tragedy here on Ares. There was a profound lesson to be learned there and as a military man I was well aware of it. I was a warrior and it rankled to consider the action I knew must be taken now. But I knew I would have to accept the bitter pill, my men and I were hopelessly outclassed. There was only one recourse.

Until today, I had been the only person on the planet Ares to have a gun. I still had my beloved .45 auto on my person, the same gun that had been transported with me to Ares when I had first come to this world so long ago. Now I realized I was the only person who held a gun on our side of this conflict against an enemy so heavily armed with high velocity rifles as to make any outcome by us against them a sad joke. It would be simple slaughter, as I had told Zaor. I wondered if I would ever see my good friend again, I wondered if I would ever see my beloved Sirah again.

"Why do we not attack, Jon Kirk?" asked Tor-nul, the captain of my Black Dragons bodyguard. He was young, fearless, and all eager. I knew he would fight and die for his emperor, as would each of the one hundred brave men under his command with him. They would fight and die, most bravely, I knew, but all for nothing, because I knew there was absolutely no chance of victory for us against these Blue Kortas.

I looked at the enemy troops form up into orderly groups. It was depressing. These Blue Korta mercenaries were nothing like the blue-skinned humans of Vognar—the Blues, or Vognars from the western continent we had fought last year. They were at least human—these Kortas were not. They were blue in skin hue but otherwise nothing about them even resembled humans. They were humanoid in shape but they looked like giant blue trolls with great white horns sprouting from the sides of their large ugly heads.

I sighed and swallowed the bitter pill. There was no other recourse.

"Make ready for a silent withdrawal, Tor-nul," I ordered sternly. I could see his face cloud with surprise at my order. "And send a messenger to Sahn-Jor. Tell him he must prepare to withdraw his troops also, as quickly as he is able. We must save the army, save our people. We are withdrawing from the Shiva Plains and will rendezvous in the secret caves of the Coastal Mountains north of Tarcos."

Tor-nul could barely believe what he had heard me say. He stood stone-still, shocked. I looked at him and put my hand upon his shoulder, "Tor-nul, do you obey your emperor?"

"Yes, of course, Jon Kirk."

"Tor-nul, do you trust in your emperor's judgment?"

"Absolutely, Jon Kirk."

"Then do as I instruct, Tor-nul, please."

Tor-nul swallowed hard, said, "Yes, My Emperor. Immediately!"

It is a hard thing to do for any fighting man to withdraw in the face of an approaching enemy as we did that day. Yet there was no other action I could take. I knew a battle here would only result in a massacre of my people. It would gain us nothing but bleed our army of our most noble warriors. I had to find another way to fight this war, but first I had to preserve our forces long enough until I found *that* way.

* * * *

The single enemy ship that had invaded our world on that lonely dusty plain that day debarked six thousand fully armed Blue Korta warriors on their dread bird-like *phar* mounts. The debarking process took many hours, time I put to good use making sure that all the warriors under my command would be long gone and out of harm's way by the time the enemy began to move his ground troops against us. I was more concerned about any airships they might bring into action. We were not ready for that yet.

My scouts brought back the bad news that the Blue Korta army had split up into six columns of one thousand warriors each, and it was not any surprise to me that each column was headed to each of the recently liberated green cities of Ares.

Our forces were now safely far away, approaching the mountains far north of the mostly empty city of Tarcos. I left behind volunteer snipers and scouts to harass the enemy as much as possible so as to make their occupation as costly as possible. They were the bravest of the brave and their actions bought us more time as our civilians and armed forces hastily withdrew to safety.

Zaor and his people had now joined us. Zaor heard the news via messenger and grew quiet, thoughtful, but he had obeyed my orders and evacuated Tarcos. I thanked the war gods of Ares for that and I hoped they were still with us.

Sahn-Jor spoke up, "They have divided their force, that is good, There are but a mere thousand of these strange blue warriors now to oppose us, Jon Kirk. I do not see them able to conquer one of our fully defended Ares cities."

I shook my head, said, "Sahn-Jor, you do not understand the weapons they possess. And there is something else, our invisibility devices do not work now. The beam emanating from the ships around Ares is jamming our devices. Without invisibility our forces cannot win."

"That changes everything, My Lord," Sahn Jor said sadly.

"We can still fight them, even though they have projectile weapons and we have no invisibility, our warriors are brave, fierce," Zaor spoke up carefully.

"Yes," I replied simply, "that is certainly true, but with their projectile weapons and without our invisibility, I have no choice in my decision. With such weapons the enemy do not need a hundred thousand—or even ten thousand warriors—to take a city or even this entire world. They can do so with a mere hundred, as they are doing. But they will not even need to do that. They have warships out in space orbiting Ares right now. They can fire down upon our cities any time they want. The destruction would be horrific. That is why I want the people to leave the cities. We will leave behind only a small force in the cities."

Zaor was silent.

Sahn-Jor said, "Jon Kirk, this is dire news indeed, can such a thing be true?"

I nodded sadly. They could see the concern in my face. "I am afraid it is all true."

"What is to be done?" Zaor asked, realizing the danger fully now.

"We are doing it," I said firmly. "You have your orders?"

Both men nodded with grim reluctance. These were honorable fighting men who champed at the bit to defend their city, they saw no honor in fleeing from an invading enemy. They did not want to run. But I knew what had to be done.

I told them sternly, "My friends, we must conserve our forces, keep our army and people intact, and be patient until we can fight our own battle, *our own way*. So for now we evacuate the Six Cities and make to the safety of the forests and mountains where even the space fleet of the enemy can not track us."

Zaor nodded reluctantly, then he and Sahn-jor left.

Tor-nul, the captain of my imperial bodyguard stood by silent and strong as ever. Ready to fight, ready to take whatever order I should give him. I could see that he desired to speak but he knew that there was nothing to be said now.

"So we desert the cities?" Ar-den, another of my trusted ministers asked with gloom. He was a wise man and one of my most important counselors. He spoke slowly and carefully with disbelief and deep sadness at what had come to pass.

I nodded. "There is nothing else to say at this point. We shall escape this Blue Korta trap, for I know that is exactly what it is, and we shall live to fight another day. I will live for that day."

"As will I, My Emperor," Tor-nul stated with solid resolve.

Ar-den simply shook his head refusing to accept my words, "Jon Kirk, there must be something we can do? I implore you. You are an outworlder, like these invaders—though I mean no disrespect in saying that—but surely your secret knowledge from your own world can counter their own secret and strange knowledge and weapons?"

I looked Ar-den in the eyes and gave him a grim smile, my hand unconsciously reaching to grasp the butt of my .45 auto where it sat holstered at my side.

I allowed a smile and said, "Ar-den, you have given me an idea! You have given me hope!"

The old sage didn't know what I meant but his face brightened in reaction to my positive words and manner.

I looked to my captain of the Black Dragons, "Tor-nul, send your best men to find old Ras-noor and all his scientists and apprentices. Have them brought to our camp in the mountains under secure guard, bring them to the Caves of Conscience."

Tor-nul saluted and made ready to immediately leave upon my order.

"…and Tor-nul," I ordered, stopping the man in his tracks before he had left the room. I reached for my .45 auto and withdrew the handgun from its holster at my side. I motioned for him to come closer and then handed him the weapon. "Tell Ras-noor we need him and his people to begin production of a projectile weapon based upon this design immediately. I want handguns, of this size, and longer guns, what are called rifles, that are long like spears. They will have rifled barrels—that means barrels with groves cut inside them, which will allow more distance and accuracy of the projectile."

"Yes, Jon Kirk!" Tor-nul held my .45 looking at it in wide-eyed fascination, almost as if it were some kind of holy relic. He had surely never seen the likes of such a thing before in his life. Swords and knives were the weapons of Ares, guns were unknown. I had hoped to keep it that way, but now there was no choice but to go to more destructive weapons. He smiled, and carefully packed my .45 away in his pouch.

"I do not understand this weapon," Tor-nul stated suspiciously.

"No need, Ras-noor will know what to do with it," I told him confidently.

Ton-nul nodded and saluted preparing to leave on his mission.

I stopped Tor-nul and gave him some .45 slugs as well, then told him, "Guard that weapon and those bullets with your life, be sure Ras-noor and his people receive them and work day and night on making our new weapons based upon this design."

"I shall have my best men find Ras-noor and give him your order. It shall be done as you wish, My Emperor!"

Once Tor-nul had gone, Ar-den approached me, "My Emperor, these are dark days upon us. What shall we do now?"

I took one last look at the magnificent throne room of Tarcos, the city so many of us had fought and died to free from the dread Winged-men. The city we had named after my wily old friend Tar-gool. I wish he was here with us now, the old scoundrel. I took one long last look at the gleaming turrets of lovely Tarcos, the mighty balustrades and spires, the muilti-columned buildings, the glory and majesty of this greatest and most beautiful of Ares cities.

"Jon Kirk?" Ar-den drew my attention from my revelry.

I sighed. I was ready. "I know. What do we do? What we do now, old friend, is we leave," I told him simply. "We leave so that we may fight another day. This is not the end for us, Ar-den, it is just the beginning and I guarantee you, there will one day come a battle this world has never seen before nor ever imagined, and we shall be victorious!"

CHAPTER 4

STRATEGIC WITHDRAWL

The coming weeks were dark and bereft of all hope and joy as six columns of *phar* mounted Blue Korta warrior cavalry occupied each of the Six Cities of the Green Empire of Ares. They came into the empty cities with their Winged-men allies—who had now come out of hiding to join them—to sack and rule over our cities once again. Our people were thankfully all gone and safe now, so the invaders only met my undercover scouts and snipers, warriors and guardsmen who fought them house to house. It was vicious warfare to tie them down and make their occupation as costly as possible. They were brave heroic men and women who laid down their lives to buy us time to prepare to meet the enemy on a more even footing. I had a plan in that regard but it would take time.

In the meantime, what was effectively martial law had been proclaimed in each of the Six Cities by the Winged-men and their Blue Korta shock troops, now that they were triumphant. Our cities were under occupation. None could oppose them. Even though not all inhabitants of the Six Cities had heeded my order to withdraw, all now knew resistance to the enemy was futile. Those that stayed behind, seeking to protect their homes, ships, farms and families were helpless and many were just cut down. Others lay cowering and hiding, awaiting the day of our victory. I hoped that day would come soon.

The wily governor of one of our cities, Kal-sar, had refused to heed my order and with his small army and a militia drafted from all the green-skinned people in his city, fought a battle to the death to hold their beloved city against an invading column of Blue Korta shock troops. Reports from the front showed it turned out to be a terrible massacre for our side. It became a battle so quickly lost none could believe it, but I believed it, for the men of Ares with their swords and spears were no match for the projectile weapons of the Blue Kortas. What began as a battle where the invaders were so heavily outnumbered, soon turned into a disaster for our brave warriors, which by the next morning became an utter massacre. It was terrible. It was rumored that Blue Korta troops and their Winged-men allies had embarked on an all out effort to exterminate the green humans of that city, and I was sure such would be their plans for the rest of the green people of the remaining cities of Ares.

Those were dark days. Meanwhile the grim business ahead was forming the remainder of the refugees from Tarcos and our other five cities—that made up our army and contained the population of all our Ares survivors—into a coherent defensive force up in the security of the mountain caves. These caves ran deep and were large, but were perfect for our protection, even keeping us safe from the weapons of the ships up in space orbiting around Ares should they be used against us. Thankfully these space weapons from the ships orbiting Ares were not used at this time.

We now set up extensive camps far away in the colder northern reaches, but we lived, we survived. There were thousands of us hiding in hundreds of the many great caverns throughout the northern mountains. We were a hundred times many hundred Greens, with some Blues joining us as allies as well. I wondered if the same situation was happening on the western continent of Vognar? Our allies there were always wary of Winged-men scouts flying overhead or Blue Korta patrols that having done their dirty work so well by scouring the Six Cities and the surrounding countryside of green-skinned Ares humans—were now looking for new conquests. Namely us—the people who had been able to escape them and their occupation.

The enemy knew our people and army were hidden somewhere in the vastness of the Northern Mountains, but as yet, our groups had remained undiscovered burrowed down deep into the cavern systems. It was a situation that I knew could not remain for much longer. We each felt as if the noose of doom was drawing more tightly around us all. Each day I feared that soon the other shoe would drop—as I rushed our people continued their work on new and better weapons.

Those dark days were the worst I had ever encountered on Ares. I had been through so much, fought and won so many battles—most of them against all odds. Through that crucible, I had accomplished much for my beloved Sirah, myself, my little son, and my adopted people. Now it all seemed lost. Or so some people thought. Now we all faced genocidal extermination at the hands of an implacable and powerful new enemy from outer space—the mysterious spacemen!

Nevertheless, I still lived—we still lived! Where there is life—anything can be possible. I knew what needed to be done. I was up to the challenge. Somehow I was determined to snatch victory from the jaws of doom.

With Sirah forever at my side on those dark days, and with good friends like Zaor, his mate Manalia, Sahn jor, Tor-nul and Ar-den, we constantly discussed, planned and schemed, seeking any way to maximize our options. Options which seemed so limited. It was, for now, galling that we had to bide our time. Remain hidden. Regroup and organize, and then train new fighters with new weapons.

New weapons were the key to any victory. I had Ras-noor and his people working night and day and I pushed the old scientist for quick results.

In the meantime I did what I could to fight back. I organized a secret guerrilla war against the Blue Kortas and Winged-men, with quick night strikes at their patrols, strongholds, camps. I used tactics I had learned from my Earther days fighting in Vietnam to make the enemy pay a terrible price for their occupation. We were able to do much damage, kill many of the enemy, steal some limited amounts of the precious Blue Korta projectile weapons. Samples of these were immediately sent to the secret caves where Ras-noor and his beleaguered scientists and apprentices worked around the clock to perfect a projectile firing weapon for our side that would stand up against the Blue Korta firepower. They also worked on other weapons. White fire beam projectors. Big ones.

As the weeks rolled on, and our situation in the mountains and caverns became more precarious, I continued to push poor old Ras-noor and his people all the harder to come up with some kind of rifle the Greens of Ares could use effectively against the Blue Korta hordes. It had to be deadly, quick to manufacture, and simple for my people to use. My main objective was to have the weapon be as simple as possible to operate.

I explained to Ras-noor the principle of point and shoot, explaining to him that a simple to use weapon would increase our firepower to eventually match that of the enemy. I did not just want to use stolen Korta rifles, I wanted us to have our own rifles, designed for effective use by the green men and women of Ares. Then as our number of weapons grew and our number of warriors grew, our army would march on the enemy, and with our vast numbers—destroy them all once and for all. But that was a long way off and there was much to do before that day's red sun would shine. The main worry I had, and the problem I had to solve before I began any attack, was the enemy warships in orbit around Ares. These would have to be dealt with before any ground offensive could be begun by my forces. To neglect those ships would be the death of us all.

Meanwhile, refugees continued to straggle into our compounds, telling us the most dire stories of death and destruction as the Kortas and their winged allies began a systematic extermination of the green people of Ares. It confirmed all our worst fears. I knew that our days were numbered unless I could change the progression of events. Now all I had to do was find some way to achieve that goal.

Often times when it appears that you are closing in upon your darkest hour, Salvation lends an intervening hand to save you from that doom-filled destiny you may fear so much. Such a situation arose one day when I felt events were closing a doom-laden net tightly around us.

"Ras-noor awaits outside, Jon Kirk," Tor-nul told me with obvious excitement. "He seeks an immediate audience."

"Have him brought forward," I instructed Tor-nul, who quickly ordered one of his officers of my bodyguard to bring the ancient Ares scientist into the make-shift audience hall—it was more than a large, but very well appointed underground cavern—it was a massive cavern I used for my headquarters and planning office these days.

I could see that wily old Ras-noor was all excitement as he came ambling forward to the huge wooden table I used as my work desk. He was followed by several of his top scientists, one each from the various fields of knowledge he used in his work. These men and women were holding quite large canvas-covered items.

"Yes, Ras-noor," I stated. "It is good to see you, old friend. What have you for us today?"

"Jon Kirk, My Emperor," he said with a smile, bowing in respect, then he approached closer unable to hold back his excitement, which had now become contagious to all in that cavern. He spurted out, "We have done it! The new wonder weapon, it is in operation and it surpasses all our wildest expectations!"

The room was silent for a bare moment with utter astonishment, it was so quiet you could hear a pin drop. Then I spoke to the old scientist.

"Now that is certainly good news! Tell me! Show us, Ras-noor!"

Ras-noor smiled, like a loving father showing off a proud child. He immediately spoke sharply to one of his younger helpers. "Ab-tor, bring forward the weapons so that the Emperor may inspect them."

I ordered the large table I used as a desk to be cleared and soon men operating under Ab-tor's directions brought over various canvas-wrapped packages. The men carefully unwrapped the objects, as everyone in the room looked on with amazement. Sirah and I held each other hopefully, I felt her tightly squeeze my hand. Zaor and his mate, Manalia, along with Sahn-jor and Tor-nul and many others looked on in rapt fascination all wondering just what was to be revealed.

Upon my old table desk were now placed three strange devices. The first two were obviously a hand gun and a rifle of some kind. I wondered just what wily old Ras-noor and his people had come up with. The handgun looked strange to me. Alien. But then again, I was on an alien world. I imagine that their Ares design made them appear much stranger and more alien than any Earth weapons. The hand gun did not look at all like my familiar .45 auto. Then there was the third device. It was something else altogether. I could plainly see that it was merely a model of some kind, a smaller representation of something... I wondered...something that was very big.

Ras-noor noticed me looking with interest at the last device.

"Jon Kirk, as you have already guessed, this last item is only a model. A significantly smaller imagining of the actual device. That actual machine is massive and has been built atop the mountain peak above my labs in the Caves of Conscience. It has already been tested and is fully operational, and ready for use."

I nodded approvingly, I would get to that later. Right now my eyes focused upon the new guns—handguns and the rifles. These were desperately needed now.

"And what of these...guns?" I asked, looking at the other two items upon the table. They certainly looked strange, a hand gun and rifle in their purpose certainly, but with baffled edges and crystal struts and circular clear ball loops around the barrel. If I didn't know better I would swear that they were some kind of ray gun right out of Buck Rogers or Flash Gordon.

Ras-noor came closer and took out something from his robes which he proffered to me. It was wrapped in cloth and when he unwrapped it I saw right away that it was my trusty old .45 auto. He handed it to me with a wry grin. I thanked him, placing the weapon back into my holster where it belonged. It was like a long-lost friend had come back to me and I was glad to have it back.

"My Lord, that is a most interesting, and if I may be so bold, dangerous device. Your—'gun', as you call it—is much like the stolen Blue Korta projectile weapons we have been able to analyze and copy. Both are primitive projectile weapons, but effective. Deadly effective because the people of Ares have no knowledge of—and do not use such weapons as these. Not yet. However, My Emperor, that does not mean that we can not manufacture such weapons as these—and perhaps weapons that may be far superior."

I looked at Ras-noor closely and smiled at the old rogue, my entire entourage and routine looked at him in awe. My officers, generals, even my wife Sirah and my best friend, Zaor were stunned by this news. What did he mean?

"Please explain, my friend," I asked quickly, bursting with curiosity and renewed hope.

Ras-noor nodded, "While your 'gun' and the Blue Korta weapons are a product of a science alien to Ares, projectile weapons are entirely effective against our swords, so we have devised a weapon using the forbidden knowledge from the ancient Book of Kor. From the long ago Ancients of Ares. My scientists and I have created something far superior in destructive force, we have been able to resurrect the knowledge that enabled us to create the dread death ray weapons of the ancients!"

Well, you can imagine that Ras-noor's disclosure pretty well shocked me and everyone in that cavern. I was not as up on Ares religious practices and history as I should have been. Here I had been hoping for some sorry imitation of an Earthlike handgun or rifle, but what I had been presented with now was a deadly death ray weapon built on the advanced scientific knowledge of the ancient people of Ares. Now this might be interesting.

Ras-noor now looked somewhat disappointed, "I am sorry, My Lord, that I was not able to synthesize your 'gun' to better effect, nor the Korta projectile weapons, as you requested. This knowledge is not familiar to us and since you stressed great speed because of our dire situation, I deemed it best to fall back upon our reliance of the ancient texts and knowledge. I am familiar with these, though I do not proclaim the fact too openly. Tar-gool tasked me with researching the ancient knowledge. I am sorry to be unable to recreate your 'gun' weapon, but if you like, we may be able to have some of them manufactured some day. It should not prove difficult, our factories are just not tooled to manufacture such items in mass amounts. I was able to recreate a sufficient supply of the short projectiles your 'gun' fires. Perhaps some day I may be able to create more of these 'guns' for you and our people to enjoy."

"Enjoy?" I asked with surprise. "It is a deadly weapon."

"Of course, it is, Jon Kirk," Ras-noor replied. "I apologize for my failure."

I looked at Ras-noor sharply and let out a long and relieved laugh as I approached him and patted him excitedly upon the back like a long-lost brother. "You think I am disappointed with you, old friend? Let me tell you, nothing could be father from the truth. You have done an outstanding job. I am in your debt. I had no idea that the ancients of Ares possessed this kind of advanced knowledge."

"Once, long ago, our world boasted a glorious and advanced civilization, but war and division among factions allowed us to grow weak. The knowledge is old and long forgotten, My Lord, by all save a few. Secret guardians keep the flame lit, but it is a low flame that has all but died out these days. The old texts are now dusty books that are never opened to be read, except by odd follows like myself."

"Well, Ras-noor, I am overjoyed and you have done your mission very well. All your people have done your jobs well. I congratulate you all. You may have saved the green people of Ares—but, well, I must ask you candidly—are you sure these weapons will work? And have you made enough of them to arm every man who wants to carry such a weapon to use against our enemy? Every woman too?"

"Why, yes, My Lord," Ras-noor smiled triumphantly. "All have been tested and work perfectly."

Then the old scientist handed me one of the new hand guns. It was quite light to the touch, apparently being made mostly out of some kind of plastic and glass. It fit comfortable in the hand, but it looked to me like a child's toy, and not a deadly weapon of war. But I had learned never to take for granted anything I encountered on this mysterious world of Ares.

I nodded, hefting the gun in my hand, it was rather light. I looked at the old scientist curiously, "And what does it do, Ras-noor?"

He smiled, then replied simply, "Why, My Lord—it destroys things."

"Explain, please," I prompted him for more detailed information.

"Well, whatever you point at and fire upon—that item if not living will explode. If the target be living tissue, it will instantly be killed by the death ray. The ray cuts into the flesh and will create a burning wound. It burns the cells, exploding them on the molecular level. The longer you hold the trigger upon the target, the more severe the wound. Hold the trigger down for enough time—just a sparse moment longer is all it takes—and the entire subject will be vaporized. It will disappear. Would you like to try it?"

"Of course," I said enthusiastically.

Now here was a real weapon!

Ras-noor made a gesture and from the end of the huge underground cavern I saw a detachment of my Black Dragons, the imperial bodyguard, approaching. My warriors held two men as prisoners between them, and as they came closer I saw who it was the warriors held. I could scarcely believe it. It was none other than Vakon and Crooch ,and they were being dragged forward in chains as befitted their ilk.

Crooch! And Vakon! The traitors! I could scarce restrain my elation at seeing these two villains having finally been caught and brought forward to receive their just punishment. I was not aware they had been taken captive, but I was overjoyed to see them here now and in chains.

Ras-noor called out an order to the lieutenant of the Black Dragons, "Chain them to the wall. They shall make excellent targets for the Emperor to test the effectiveness of his new weapons!"

I scarcely knew what to think about this. My eyes just bored into Crooch with a hatred I could scarce believe I possessed. These two had betrayed me many times in the past. Their treachery knew no bounds. It was an ugly darkness within me, something I must say that quite surprised me and that I was not proud of—in spite of all their treachery against me, my beloved Sirah, and our people. I wanted them to die.

Zaor quickly interjected, "Jon Kirk, may I speak with you for a moment about these two men?"

I knew what was bothering Zaor, for I felt the same feeling within me, so I waited and when he approached me I asked him what he had on his mind.

"My Lord, these men have not been captured, they walked into our camp unarmed and of their own accord. They said they have come to aid our cause and have told me that they possess valuable information you will need to hear," Zaor informed me seriously.

I looked at Zaor unable to hide my astonishment at his words.

"Is this true?" I asked incredulous.

I saw Zaor and Ras-noor both nod in the affirmative.

I sighed, then asked for Vakon and Crooch to be brought forward.

The two prisoners were brought closer to me, still covered in their chains. I saw Sirah look upon them with an ill-confined blood-lust and loathing. I could not blame her, for these men had wronged her terribly, wronged us all.

"This story does not sound at all like the actions of the Vakon or the Crooch I know," I said gruffly, dubious in the extreme. I could never forget their treachery, abduction, murder plots. "It is not like these two men to contribute aid to anyone. They are self-serving and treacherous."

"No, it does not sound like them at all, Jon Kirk. I agree with you," Zaor said firmly, "but for the right price…"

I nodded, "Now that sounds more like them. But what do they have that I could possibly need, Zaor?"

"If I may be allowed to speak, Jon Kirk?"

"What?" I asked, turning my head to look upon the man who had just spoken. The very sight of him revolted me.

Now my eyes bored into the two prisoners with a flare of bright fire, but then I calmed down and observed them more carefully. There was something to this I needed to know.

It was Crooch, chained and bound but speaking boldly before me. He said, "I and my companion, Vakon here, have no love for the Winged-men of Zar, and far less for these vile alien Blue Kortas. We have no wish to be exterminated, as I am sure you are aware by now is the plan they have for every member of the entire green race. There is no dealing with them…"

"And I am sure you have tried!" I stated, allowing my anger to show.

Crooch gave me a slight grin, "Yes, we did try, but there is no dealing with them, no—compromise. Though I and Vakon here can ill understand it, they are quite rigid in this new policy and of course it has presented severe difficulties and complications for my companion and myself. And since our past… ah, difficulties…with you and your noble cause of fighting for Ares freedom…"

"Cut the crap!" I growled, brimming over with anger at the fiend's boldness and slick, slimy talk. Of course I did not use the word 'crap' but instead the Ares equivalent *sloss*, meaning garbage. "Crooch, I would have you drawn and quartered right now, or perhaps used as a target for Ras-noor's death ray weapon, had not Zaor told me that you and Vakon came here of your own free will and possess certain information I might find valuable. You had better hope that is the case. So start talking and remember that your lives depend upon the importance of that information."

"We understand. Indeed we do have such information," slavered Vakon, who spoke up now and was immediately nudged to silence by Crooch, who seemed the master of the two.

"My Lord Kirk," Crooch cooed softly, "I made a terrible mistake years ago and wish to rectify that now by offering you what information we possess. Information on the source of these alien Blue Kortas and about the Secret Empire of The Hundred Worlds of which they represent."

There was absolute silence throughout the huge cavern. Even Ras-noor and his eager scientists were silent and listening.

"What information?" I demanded, "and how did you come by it?"

Crooch bowed, "If I may be allowed…" He rattled his chains in evident discomfort and motioned to his companion sadly.

I nodded, deciding to play the game only so long and so far as there was something to be gained for our cause.

"Zaor, I think I will have those two released from their chains, but make sure they are watched carefully."

I looked at Vakon and Crooch sharply, "One crooked treacherous move, one untoward look, and my archers will cut you down. Or perhaps I will shoot you myself with this new heat beam weapon."

"Yes, My Lord," Crooch crooned offering up an oily smile of gratitude. "We thank you for your gracious mercy."

"Hah!" I barked gruffly. "Get on with it!"

Crooch did not reply but I thought I saw the hint of a triumphant leer flick across his lips.

I looked at the two men carefully and hoped that I would not regret this decision, but I knew that if these two fiends had come here of their own free will—they were not only here to *offer* me information—I was sure they were here because they *wanted* something as well. What did they want? Their lives? I thought not, since they had been free and had given up that freedom to come here. They had done this of their own free will. No, there was something else. Something much more devious lurking in the black pit of their villainous minds. I wondered what it could be. I had to find out.

Sahn-jor came over to me and whispered carefully, "Jon Kirk, these men should be executed immediately for all the trouble they have fermented, not released. They are too dangerous."

I looked at my First Minster with surprise. He was the least violent of men, a peaceful man, a man who had even negotiated peace with the vile Zaran Grusus one year ago, but I knew he was a very practical man as well. He did not mince words. If even *he* thought these men should be put to death…?

"Perhaps you are correct, Sahn-jor, they certainly deserve such a fate, but I want to hear what they have to say first," I replied firmly. I motioned for Zaor to have his men release Vakon and Crooch from their chains. Once the chains were taken off the two looked at me and smiled, their evil faces trying to look grateful.

"Thank you, Master," Vakon muttered.

Without further delay I demanded, "Now out with it! What is this story you speak of? What is this Secret Empire of The Hundred Worlds and how does it effect us here on Ares?"

CHAPTER 5

THE SECRET EMPIRE OF THE HUNDRED WORLDS

"My Lord," Crooch began carefully, and apparently in all candor now, "my companion and I have seen many wonders and many terrible things in our brief aliment with the Winged-men—though none so terrible as these Blue Korta monsters from outer space —and their even more terrible masters."

I nodded, waiting, wanting specifics, facts, and impatient to get them, "Continue. I know the invaders here are from off-planet, not from Ares. But where exactly are they from? What do they want?"

Crooch wrung his hands nervously and smiled, then he continued, "From what we learned there is an empire of worlds out among the planets of the upper sky, beyond the sky even, what is called outer space. It is an enormous empire, in some ways like the Winged-men of Zar once held sway in their empire here over this planet of Ares. Only this outer space empire is made up of one hundred worlds, only one of them being Zar—home of the Winged-men."

I nodded. "Continue."

"This empire is called The Secret Empire of The Hundred Worlds, and sometimes known simply as The Secret Empire, for those few who know that it even exists. It rules many hundreds, if not thousands of planets much like our own that exist throughout the infinities of known space. It is mind-boggling, immense, inconceivable, but it exists nonetheless. They hold sway over any world where there are people and riches, but few if any of the inhabitants of the planets they rule really know about them. They stay quite, unseen and mostly unknown in the background, and they rule from behind the scenes through surrogates, like the fiends from Zar rule here on Ares."

"Ruled," I corrected firmly.

Crooch looked at me carefully, allowing a thin leering grin.

I added, "The Winged-men once ruled Ares, but no longer do, and never will again."

Crooch nodded, smiled at me oily, "Of course, My Lord. We all hail your great victories. Regardless, none of the local inhabitants of these occupied worlds ever dream the truth. There really is a Secret Empire. And only one of these hundred worlds—but only *one*—is Zar, the original home of the Winged-men."

"That is all very interesting," Sahn-jor replied, looking intently at Crooch with ill-concealed contempt, still not being able to get over the man's treachery and the penalty he desired for the man and his partner in crime, "but we have determined most of this already. Tell us something we do not know?"

"And how do you even know this information?" I demanded, for while we knew some of what Crooch had told us, it had taken us a long while to find out this information, mainly from Blue Korta prisoners. But I wondered how did Crooch know this information?

Wily Crooch bristled but continued with his story, rising to the challenge, "At this point in time almost one hundred such warships of space, much like that single ship that landed on the Shiva Plains near the River Afar are making a circle about Ares."

"Orbit," I stated. "They are in orbit."

Crooch looked up at me, smiled and said, "Yes, I believe that is the term I have heard them use, that is correct, for you are also an outworlder. I almost forgot that fact."

"I did not think that the wily Crooch ever forgets much."

"Indeed, Jon Kirk," he grimaced, squirming and obviously uncomfortable now.

"So what of these one hundred warships? Our scientists, Ar-den and Ras-noor have spotted them by using our enhanced vision devices, so we know they are there. Why and what do they intend?"

"One such of these warships was used to bring Ares to its knees in the re-conquest of the planet for those of Zar," Crooch said carefully, then looking about the massive cavern for maximum effect, "but did you know that the other ninety-nine space vessels are waiting to meet and do battle with some other enemy space force that is even now approaching? Jon Kirk, did you know that the warships of The Secret Empire of The Hundred Worlds have their own deadly enemy to deal with? Do you not see the possibilities…?"

That was new information indeed, and possibly valuable, though what I could do with it I had no idea as yet. I thought on it carefully, then nodded. This was valuable information, but just what did it mean and what use could I make of it to free the people of Ares? "Among the people of my world, Crooch, it is sometimes said that the enemy of my enemy, is my friend."

Crooch mulled those words over for a moment. I could see he was savoring the phrase. "A most interesting maxim, I like it, Jon Kirk."

"I thought you would. You are a man with a treacherous bent who would appreciate such twisted logic. Now who are these new players? What are they called? What are they like? I want information." I asked impatiently. "And what do they want?"

"My companion, Vakon, and I were not able to discover too much about them, My Lord. They are mysterious. We have surely not discovered as much information about them as we would have liked. However, we do know that these ones we call the Newcomers are deeply hated by the Hundred Worlders, who seem to be terrified of the threat they pose. Even the Blue Kortas tremble at the thought of going up against these Newcomers in battle."

I looked at my officers and ministers, then to my beloved Sirah, who nodded at me with her own brand of grim determination. We were deep in it now, as the old expression went, and it seemed to be getting deeper.

"Jon Kirk, the Newcomers have an empire made up of various… beings, but they do not talk at all like us, nor look like us, not exactly," Crooch stopped not knowing how to explain aliens in Ares terms, but I understood it only too well. So they were aliens but some were humanoid—others…? I wondered what this new threat, this Enemy Empire, or Newcomers, would be like if it put the fear of death in such brutal creatures as the Blue Kortas and their masters!

"So we have an Enemy Empire, or these Newcomers, that are bringing their warships to do battle with the warships of The Secret Empire of The Hundred Worlds. And in the middle of it all is tiny Ares. And us!" I growled. It was one real deadly mess. I knew tiny Ares and its people would be swept aside like a giant would swat an annoying fly, without even a single thought in such a war between two such powerful enemies. However, I also knew that there might be possibilities here to play one enemy against the other. If it could be done? But could it be done? And if so, how?

Crooch nodded, allowing a wry grin, "Such are the complications of the situation as we know them presently."

The treacherous one's companion, Vakon, added, "The Secret Empire sent one warship here to take back Ares for the winged creatures of Zar, just one warship because they see us as no threat, they call us primitives. We are no threat. It is an insult. For them we are an easy conquest. Or re-conquest. The projectile weapons of their Blue Korta shock troops are so devastating that no green warrior could ever hold up against them with mere swords or axes. It is insulting to our warrior's honor. Our enemy only needed the use of just one of their mighty warships from space to conquer your Six Cities and our entire world. It is a disgrace."

"You sound like a patriot, Vakon," I said cynically.

"On this matter, I suppose I am."

I nodded, "Be that as it may, we have surmised as much and made some preparations."

Ras-noor and his group of scientists had stood on the side listening to Crooch and his partner's words, now I motioned for him to come forward.

"Jon Kirk," Ras-noor offered, "these enemy warships of The Secret Empire of The Hundred Worlds, this so-called Secret Empire—which is not a secret any longer—do pose a serious threat to us and Ares. Do you want me to use our death ray against their orbiting warships? Our weapons can blow them out of the sky."

I shot a sharp look towards Ras-noor. "You can do that with your ray weapon? Is this true! You can shoot those huge ships that are so far away out of the sky in orbit?"

Ras-noor smiled and picked up the ray rifle and brought it forward. "With your permission, My Lord, a small demonstration."

I nodded, "Please proceed."

Ras-noor pointed to a life-size marble statue of an ancient Ares warrior at the other end of the great cavern. He picked up the ray weapon, pointed the muzzle at the statue and pressed the trigger. There was a slight sound as if of whooshing and an instantaneous ray of bright light focused on the statue for a spilt second—then the statue exploded into a hundred tiny fragments!

Only dust remained.

"It is gone!" Zaor shouted in disbelief.

A roar of astonishment and then wild cheers rang throughout the cavern from all who were there to see this wondrous event. I even saw Crooch and Vakon smile at what they had just seen.

"Incredible!" Sahn-jor exclaimed jubilantly.

"Of course, were the subject living flesh, it would be burned, wounded, and soon killed, depending on how long you hold down the trigger upon the firing mechanism. The time it takes to wound an enemy is but a split second. Hold the trigger for a bare moment longer and the entire subject will be vaporized by the ray and altogether disappear," Ras-noor explained with a wry grin. There was great pride now shown in his features at his successful work.

Everyone in the huge cavern had seen the demonstration but could not entirely believe what their eyes had shown them. It was truly amazing.

Was it some kind of magic? I knew it was not, but many of my people thought that it was. They had surely never seen the likes of this before.

"No, this is not some magic," I told them explaining, "it is a super weapon created by our scientists from the old knowledge of the long buried Ares Ancients. The death ray works! It is a devastating weapon we can now use against our enemies."

I nodded at Ras-noor, and he nodded back at me with a wide smile upon his face. That one simple acknowledgement from me to him was all the thanks he needed for what he had accomplished—something that was far beyond my own dreams. His face shown with happiness.

So did I. Now we had a real chance to fight the enemy on equal terms. The game had now changed!

Ras-noor put down the rifle. He approached me like some little old toymaker whose latest invention had exceeded all expectations. "My Lord, we can do the same thing to the enemy space vessels, by using the larger ray projectors we have built atop these mountains. They are ready and set to use, awaiting your order."

Now I saw real possibilities. Now I saw hope.

CHAPTER 6

THE ENEMY FLEET

I disbursed the audience. I told Sahn-jor to take away Crooch and Vakon and keep a close eye on them. No chains, but I still wanted them placed in a secure locked cell and guarded day and night.

In the meantime, Zaor and I had an intensive and private meeting with Ras-noor and the scientists who were his department heads, to plot our future use of these wonderful weapons, and to determine just how we were going to use them against our enemies. We spoke for many hours, much of it in heated debate.

I closed the meeting by telling them, "Gentlemen, these are weapons I never hoped for, but will gladly use to free Tarcos, and our other cities from the Winged-men and these Blue Korta invaders. And we will blow the warships of The Secret Empire of the Hundred Worlds—this so-called Secret Empire—we will blow their warships out of the sky."

Ras-noor nodded, "We only await your word, My Lord."

Zaor spoke up then, "I would think carefully upon this, Jon Kirk. Yes, we should free the Six Cities, defeat the Winged-men once and for all, and destroy these Blue Korta invaders and the ship they came in here upon Ares, but I would think more deeply about attacking their space fleet."

"How so, Zaor?" I asked curiously, for he was ever for going ahead with battle and did not often sanction caution.

"Well, if these Newcomers do indeed exist—if it is true we have another fleet of warships coming to fight the ships orbiting around Ares—I am thinking perhaps we should not interfere with their coming battle? Even better, let them fight it out between themselves. Then if need be, we can destroy the winner."

I looked at Zaor with a big smile. "I like this."

Zaor continued, "If we destroy the fleet presently orbiting Ares, then once this Newcomer fleet reaches Ares, I wonder what they will do? Will they go away? No, they will see us as a powerful new threat and they will attack Ares. They may see us a greater threat if we are the victors. I am concerned we may be replacing one enemy with another and that it may not be wise for us to show our new super weapons to our enemies so soon."

I nodded, Zaor's words made sense. I said, "Then it is settled, we will use our death ray rifles here on Ares to destroy the Winged-men and Blue Kortas, and destroy or capture the one ship that has landed on the Shiva Plain. We will hold back use of the larger platform weapons until we have more information on the fleets orbiting Ares, and the outcome of their battle."

Ras-noor smiled, "Wise planning, My Lord."

"We hold back our most powerful weapon until it is needed," Zaor stated simply.

"I agree, this way we don't show all our cards at once," I stated, though neither Ras-noor or Zaor, nor their captains knew the meaning of that Earthly saying. I would have to explain the game of poker to them one day. I smiled. It was pay-back time now. But this would have to be done the right way to be successful.

"Ras-noor, I want you and your people to expand production on as many of these hand and rifle ray weapons as possible. Spare nothing. I want your people working day and night, take whatever you need. We need at least ten thousand of these weapons by the time the next red sun sets. And I want not one—but two dozen of the large mountaintop gun emplacements to be built and ready to use by then as well. More if you can give them to me. Then we'll shake up the Blue Kortas and their Secret Empire masters right to the core."

"They won't know what hit them!" Zaor said proudly.

"And that will be just the beginning," I added. "Now, gentlemen, move it!"

* * * *

The next few weeks were hectic and troublesome. I knew we had to play our cards carefully, making it appear we were still hiding and fearful of the Winged-men scouts and Blue Korta patrols. In the meantime, our own spies and scouts checked the strength of the enemy, their deployment, and gathered a wealth of valuable information preparatory to our attack.

While all this was going on our people kept low and out of sight while Ras-noor and his team spared no expense to make sure our warriors had the weapons they would need, when they needed to be used.

I put Zaor in charge of training our fighters and warriors in the use of the new weapons—a rifle which would make each of our warriors all but invincible. Those men and women he trained, later trained others, and so on. And even though we did not have the full amount of weapons yet in hand, the training progressed well and each fighter knew what to do when the time came.

* * * *

Three weeks later, the web of the Winged-men and their Blue Korta shock troops began to close tightly around our hiding place in the Northern Mountains as I knew that it would. A patrol comprising five hundred units of Kortas with Winged-men auxiliaries flying as scouts—each one of them armed with their own deadly projectile weapon—was moving quickly at us from the dry sea basin below the foothills of the mountains where we were hiding in refuge. It was a large force of Blue Kortas, and they no doubt felt secure with their superior weapons and winged allies scouting the skies for them for the location of our hiding places. They were looking for caves in the mountainsides. I did not want to do anything to alarm them out of their feeling of superiority and security.

"One more day, My Lord," Tor-nul told me, apprehensive, but as ever eager for battle. "Then they will be here. Their flying scouts—those damnable Winged-men—will soon discover these caverns and our refuge. Soon they will be moving their warriors in for the kill."

I nodded, "Then they shall receive a great surprise, Tor-nul. Are you ready?"

Tor-nul smiled, "I am always ready, My Lord."

* * * *

The assemblage surrounding me contained the leaders of the Green Empire government in exile and all those who had fought for Ares freedom with me to defeat the Winged-men beginning years ago. First of them all, to my right was my beloved wife, Sirah, and beside her our two best friends and my ablest general, Zaor—and his wife, Manalia. Then there were stalwarts, wise Sahn-jor, old but reliable Ras-noor, young eager Tor-nul the captain of my Black Dragons bodyguard, and Ar-men with his armed force of scouts who had proved most useful to getting us the information we needed about the enemy forces. Ar-men was running a quite effective spy and scout system.

"One more day and they shall be here," Zaor offered quietly in warning.

I said, "Sahn-jor, Ras-noor, it is time you made your reports."

Sahn-jor stood up first, this big man and ablest of administrators told me, "Jon Kirk, all is in readiness. The army has been armed with Ras-noor's new wonder ray weapons, truly magnificent devices, and all our men and women are trained and eager to use them on our enemies. Anxious, I might add, to reek revenge upon those enemies."

"And the fortifications?" I asked sharply.

"Even as we speak, our forces are moving into position along the base of the Caves of Conscience, and along the rim of the valley basin below us. Once the enemy patrol enters—we will spring the trap. It will be quick and deadly for our enemy, butchery to be sure, but nothing that they do not deserve. Our new death ray will put their projectile weapons to shame. They can not stand up against the might of Ras-noor's beam weapons. Their defeat will be guaranteed."

There were nods of approval and smiles of joy from everyone in that room, and the look of hope began to spread from face to face. It was the culmination of the desire, finally, for us to take revenge for all the Blue Korta atrocities against the people of the Six Cities that made up the Green Empire of Ares. All those who had not been lucky to escape extermination by this vicious enemy wanted payback now.

"And you , Ras-noor? How comes the work on the large death ray projectors?"

Ras-noor raised his old and obviously tired body to its full height as he stood to make his report. He looked older now, worn down, the work had taken much out of him but he had never complained one word in all those weeks.

"Jon Kirk, it is my pleasure to report to you, and the good people in this room, that we have no less than twenty full-field death ray projectors all set in hardened sites throughout these mountains. Right now, their aim is set upon the coordinates of the advancing Blue Korta force, and could cause our enemy total destruction before they are even able to close in battle with our forces. Should you decide to use them."

I thought hard on this news, looked over towards Zaor. He shook his head in the negative. "I think we will hold off on using those projectors for now, Ras-noor, I want to save them to surprise the war-ships orbiting Ares when the proper time comes."

"Of course, My Lord."

"Zaor you will lead our troops against the Blue Korta force, spring the trap and take them down with the death ray rifles. I do not want the large weapons used, or discovered by our enemies—not just yet."

Zaor nodded eagerly, ready for battle.

"It shall be done," Ras-noor added.

"That is good to hear, my friend. So then, Ras-noor, tell me more about these large death ray projectors?"

"They will immediately be re-sighted and set to fire upon the en-emy warships in orbit around Ares. I will have all in readiness so that we can shoot any space ship out of the sky upon your order. However, if there is a way to get exact coordinates of each ship, that will ensure a much more deadly result from these large beam projectors."

"That is good, I will remember that, but you remember to fire only upon my order, Ras-noor," I stated carefully. "I want to see how things transpire when that second fleet enters the space around our world. But for now, our warriors will fight and win a great victory by surprising the Kortas and Winged-men with a trap and give them a battle they never would have believed possible. It will be our first victory in this new war against our enemies!"

A wild applause ringing with cheers went up throughout the huge cavern. Victory finally appeared to be within our grasp. It would be the first battle in a long series of battles, but it would be a victory and we needed a victory desperately just then.

In a dark corner, unseen by all, I was surprised to see Vakon and Crooch nod to themselves and speak in furtive whispers. What were they doing here? Zaor was gone, he had been in charge of these pris-oners but now he had gone away to lead our forces in the forthcoming battle. What were these two about? I called over Tor-nul and put it to him.

"What are Vakon and Crooch doing here? Why have they been released?"

"Zaor allowed them out of their jail cell, in exchange for further information they gave him," Tor-nul stated simply. "I was against it, but Zaor thought it might prove a better decision to allow them some freedom—and watch them. We are watching them carefully. Then we can see who they speak with, what they are planning. There is no way they can escape these caverns without our men catching them, and even if they wanted to leave, where would they go? There is no place on Ares safe for them any longer."

"I understand but I don't like it, Tor-nul. I want you to have them both closely watched. Get your best men, hand pick them yourself from my Black Dragons, and have them stick to these two traitors like ticks on a dog."

Tor-nul nodded, then looked at me with a wide grin, "Ticks on a dog, My Lord? Another of your interesting Earther expressions?"

"Yes, but just keep your guards close to those two. I want to know where they go, who they talk to, and what they do. I will expect a report every morning."

CHAPTER 7

BATTLE AND BETRAYAL

The Battle of The Bloody Basin began the next morning. Surrounded by my commanders, with all our troops were in place hidden from the approaching enemy and we patiently waited as the Blue Korta column advanced to our positions. They were close, but still not fully within the trap yet. Once they were in the killing zone, I would give Zaor the order to spring the trap we had worked so hard to set for them, and that would begin their destruction and defeat. Or such we hoped would be the result.

Blue Korta shock troops looked barbarous and deadly as they rode upon their huge bird-like *phars*, riding boldly through the flat valley basin towards the foothills where our hidden troops awaited them behind cover of trees and large rocky boulders. They were a brutal and barbaric group of huge blue mutant humanoids, especially bred for war, their horned heads gave them a most menacing look. Even with all that, they were worse even than they looked. More deadly, more vicious, a relentless fighting force!

And yet with all that, if my plan worked here today, they would be defeated and that would hopefully be the first of many such defeats for them.

I watched with eager anticipation as the enemy boldly rode into our trap with arrogant confidence. And why not? None of them had ever lost a battle before. They were, an as yet, undefeated enemy and such gives warriors great over-confidence. As yet none of them knew what we had in store for them, but soon they would find out. Their flying scouts did not find our hidden bands of warriors, which were shielded by vision from any flyers above us. Any of their scouts that came in the direction of our positions were quietly and efficiently shot out of the sky with deadly arrows by my archers, or killed with ray beam weapons by our best sharpshooters before they ever got near our positions or saw anything to report back to their masters.

On the right and left flank I had positioned two bands of one thousand warriors, each man armed with a deadly death ray rifle. Zaor commanded the men on the right flank, Sahn-jor those on the left. Both of these generals were with their men awaiting my command to open fire and attack.

However, before that would happen, our twenty secreted large death ray projectors were sighted upon the enemy spaceships orbiting our planet to ensure no interference from that quarter. I did not anticipate any attack upon us from space as yet, for I was sure the enemy did not feel we were worth the effort, but I felt it would be prudent to be ready just in case. The men controlling those weapons were waiting to hear for my order to fire. For now, they were to stand by, stay ready, but not fire while the battle here on Ares was underway.

Ar-men stood beside me as my second in command of our own mounted shock troops, my brave Black Dragons cavalry that I would lead personally in a sweep down into the valley to cut into the enemy force once the trap had been sprung. There would be no way for any of these invading creatures to escape today. Even the flying monsters, should they try to fly away and escape, were to be brought down with arrows by our excellent archers, or if necessary, warriors using ray beam rifles.

"Jon Kirk, the enemy is drawing closer. We should spring the trap now."

"Give them another moment, Ar-men."

We waited impatiently. My heart beat loudly in my chest as the seconds passed by so slowly. It was the longest moment in my life and probably in the history of the planet Ares. It was the moment that would determine if my adopted world, and the world of my beloved wife, Sirah, our son Alun, and all our friends and comrades in arms would be free once and for all. I found myself wishing that wily old Tar-gool was still alive and here to view what would happen here today—which for good or ill would be a battle like no other. He would have appreciated the spectacle. However, I contented myself with the old Ares proverb that the dead are never truly dead on Ares, but live elsewhere and see all from the Afterworld. I hoped Tar-gool was watching the forthcoming battle from wherever he was now. I was sure that he was.

"Jon Kirk?" Ar-men prompted me softly.

I nodded, "Yes, Ar-men, it is time. Give the signal to Zaor and Sahn-jor to begin their attacks."

With the signal given, two thousand fiery death rays silently and suddenly burned brightly from two thousand places of concealment with a thunderous whoosh, hitting the Blue Korta column and their winged scouts with fiery burning explosions, There was a shudder among the enemy column, dozens, then hundreds of the enemy fell with brutal burn wounds, many others just disappeared. Instantly vaporized. More screamed out, trying to fight back, but our death rays were inflicting massive damage upon them, even thought they fought back bravely using their projectile weapons to good effect—their weapons proved no match for our own. Their armor did not protect them from our beam weapons, and even though we could not use our invisibility devices any longer because of the space ray beacon, we did not need it here and now. My men killed the enemy soldiers in what was becoming a wholesale slaughter—the same type of warfare the Blue Kortas and Winged-men made upon the Greens in every city on Ares.

Ar-men just stared in open-mouthed awe at the massive power our men held in their hands and the sheer destructive force their weapons unleashed upon the enemy.

My beloved Sirah, who stood next to me, held my hand tightly, "So it begins, my beloved?"

I reached my arm around her and kissed her gently, then said, "Yes, so we begin, my love, what I hope will be the last battle to bring us peace."

We hugged and kissed quickly. Then I broke our embrace as a detachment of my Black Dragons took Sirah and Manalia back to the safety of the caves so they would not be exposed to the dangers of the battle. I would not have them here if somehow things went wrong. When the women had been whisked away to safety, I looked over at my officers. They were all ready and eager.

"Now, Jon Kirk, it is time! The enemy has taken the measure of our death ray weapons and want none of it, they are preparing to retreat," Ar-men shouted full of excitement and bloodlust. "Let us cut tem off and finish it!"

I nodded to Ar-men, "Signal Zaor and Sahn-jor to attack. Have them bring their forces out to trap the enemy and prevent their escape."

"Yes, My Lord," Ar-men replied, sending the signal.

"Tor-nul, ready our men here for the charge. Now we go to finish the job!"

My Black Dragons were ready and champing at the bit to attack and now I gave that order.

I shouted, "Charge!" and my host of five hundred mounted Ares warriors, backed up by Tor-nul with his mounted troops of my imperial bodyguard, The Black Dragons, charged out of the Northern foothills down upon the devastated Blue Korta horde.

We hit them hard, full on at the head of their column. Instantly all was shambles and chaos among them. The Winged-men allies of the Korta horde immediately saw the trap they were now in and that the ends of it were quickly shutting upon them. Those few remaining alive in the vanguard panicked and flew away. Even as they did, our scouts and sharpshooters shot them out of the sky with our new death ray weapons. Most were hit full-on and instantly obliterated and disappeared. Some who were hit partially on an appendage, or struck with a light wound on a wing, fell to the ground in a winged burning crash. These few were rounded up by our ground troops and taken prisoner, as were some Blue Kortas who surprised us by throwing down their rifles and simply giving up. They had seen the force of our weapons and wanted no part of them. That was a surprise but they were taken captive to be questioned later for whatever information they possessed.

In the meantime I watched as Zaor and Sahn-Jor's forces attacked the rest of the Korta troops, our men coming in from the left and right flanks as planned, a pincer movement that effectively closed in upon their column and closed off any escape of the Blue Korta horde. Even now my green warriors were using their death ray rifles firing furiously, shooting down Korta troops who were desperately trying to defend themselves and break a hole in our lines to escape. Their projectile weapons were deadly but no match for our death ray rifles. It was an impossible feat for the Kortas to achieve escape now. The shoe was on the other foot for them today, for now they were the ones who were hopelessly outclassed by the super-science left to us by the ancients of Ares. It was just a matter of time until the entire Blue Korta horde was wiped out to a man—save only those few we kept as prisoners. It was all happening very fast. As the seconds passed, their time quickly ran out.

I gave the final order, "Ar-men, it is time to tighten the noose and end it. We will show them the same mercy they have shown our people in the Six Cities."

Ar-men nodded gravely, then gave the signal that ordered Zaor and Sahn-jor to move in and crush the few Kortas that were left alive. Suddenly thousands of Ares green warriors, each firing a deadly death ray rifle, ran forward in an attack on the remaining Korta force that had clumped together in what was left of their long column of soldiers. That last fight was desperate and bloody, but thankfully short, as the last of the Winged-men and Kortas was soon wiped out. Of those brave enemies who fought us to the last, not one surrendered, so not one survived.

When it was done a cheer went up as the last one of the Blue Korta shock troops fell down dead to the blood drenched ground of Ares.

I heard the shouts and chants of "Victory!" and "Death to the invaders!" and my favorite of all, "We are Free! Ares is free!"

I knew that last slogan was a bit premature but I never realized just how premature it was until I saw the mysterious airship fly overhead.

We all saw it at the same time. It wasn't the huge Blue Korta troop ship of the Secret Empire that had landed upon the Shiva Plains, nor was it any type of Blue Vognar or Kevan black ship, nor any large mother ship—it was some kind of fast, sleek scout flier, or more likely some type of rapid spy vessel. We all watched it from our valley battlefield as it flew out of the mountains behind us quickly into the upper atmosphere to leave the planet.

What now? What was this?

There was shock and consternation in the ranks, for the men saw it as some type of spy ship which was an ill omen indeed.

I saw Zaor riding over to me from the other end of the battlefield. With the battle over and won, it was just a matter of cleaning up now and caring for the few wounded. We had some casualties, but had come off very well.

"What does that ship mean, Jon Kirk?" Zaor asked as he rode up to me. I knew he was wondering about the mysterious airship as were we all. I didn't know what to make of it or what to tell him, but I knew that it could not mean anything good. I had never seen such a sleek ship before, so what was it? Was it another enemy? Some watcher or spy ship of this Enemy Empire? If so, why? The questions seemed endless and I had no answers, for myself, nor for Zaor.

"I do not know, my friend," I said at last, I was out of answers for the moment.

My concern was confirmed a moment later when Far-nor, my major-domo raced up to me on his mount shouting and gesticulating wildly. What was he doing here and away from the caves?

Tor-nul and some of his men brought Far-nor over to me, trying to calm the hysterical man and get some sense out of his words.

"Far-nor!" I shouted, "Get control of yourself! What has happened? Report!"

Far-nor made a valiant effort to control himself, and then lost his composure and broke down into tears. I had never seen the man act like this before and a sudden cold chill overtook me. Now what horror could this mean? But through his sobs and tears I could make out his words and they sent a dull terror through me.

"Oh, My Lord, Jon Kirk..." Far-nor stammered, "I tried... We all did... No one expected such treachery at the very moment of our greatest victory... of our winning the battle... No one expected such a thing at all..."

I looked at the man and my guts churned with terror. "What now? Speak, Far-nor!"

"Out with it, man!" Tor-nul barked.

Far-nor tried to gain control of himself, whimpering, "It was terrible... A raid by the enemy. A secret spy ship. And the treachery—for they had allies amongst us..."

"Vakon and Crooch!" I barked in rage grasping the poor man before me roughly.

Far-nor nodded tearfully, "Yes, My Lord, they stole the prototype of our death ray weapon and they kidnapped old Ras-noor with their Winged-men and Blue Korta allies from their mysterious spy ship."

I shook my head in rage, this could not be happening now. I shook with anger, my heart now full of fire. I felt a madness I had never felt within me before. I steeled my nerves, calm, almost too calm, scary calm.

I said softly, "Well, then, so it was Vakon and Crooch who think they can get away with our secrets? We still have the platform projectors, we'll shoot all those enemy ships out of the sky."

"But, but... My Lord, you can not do that!"

I froze. I looked at the man carefully.

"Why, Far-nor?" I looked at him, a dreadful feeling coming over me.

"Because Vakon and Crooch also stole away Manalia... and the Lady Sirah!" Far-nor added with painful reluctance.

I froze, "Sirah?"

"It can not be!" Tor-nul shouted. "She was under guard, My Lord! The Lady Manalia as well! They were taken back to the safety of the caves!"

Far-nor nodded and only mumbled sadly, "Crooch said he took them knowing you would never use the platform projectors on The Secret Empire ships with your beloved mate as a hostage on those ships."

I screamed in bloody rage and blind madness as I promised I would punish those two creatures if I had to follow them all the way to the end of Ares—or to the end of the universe itself—to free Manalia and my beloved Sirah.

CHAPTER 8

GORM

Of course once I calmed down and thought about it I realized that there appeared nothing that I could do right away to save my beloved Sirah. Nor Zaor's mate, Manalia. All this bluster, anger, it was all easier said then done. The more I thought about things, the more I realized what I had to do. It seemed incredible and virtually impossible. Far-nor's words meant that I would have to find some way to get off-planet and onto The Secret Empire warship where Sirah and Manalia were now being held. Whichever ship that was. A sound idea in theory, but in practice practically verging upon the impossible. How could I ever accomplish such a feat? I was full of despair, but I was also full of anger and an unrelenting desire to save my beloved and crush the enemy—and finally mete out just punishment to Vakon and Crooch. They both had much to answer for.

I had to deal with Vakon and Crooch's treachery now because of my mercy and reckless foolishness in not having them immediately put to the sword as Sahn-jor had advised me. Why had I not listened to him? I should have known that a snake never changes it's nature. Now Sirah, and poor Manilia and Zaor, have all paid dearly for my soft heartedness.

Nevertheless, these desires, as heartfelt and furiously as they burned within my raging breast, were not that simple to put into operation. First of all, our biggest impediment—we had no spaceship. Not a one. So there was no way of reaching the orbiting vessels of The Secret Empire fleet that circled Ares.

Even worse now, with Ras-nor, our most able scientist now in the hands of the enemy, my best chance to rescue Sirah seemed lost. I had counted on Ras-nor and his genius, his mysterious devices and long-lost knowledge from the lost Book of Kor, but now with him gone, I was at a loss to replace him. His knowledge was essential to any plan I had to save our women. He might have been able to modify one of the Vognar airships for interplanetary use given time, but now I was not sure if we had anyone with that knowledge among our scientists. If that was true I would be unable to reach Sirah to even make an attempt to save her. Frankly, at this point, I did not know what to do and I feared I would never be able to save my beloved wife. She was now effectively out of my reach and the thought burned within my mind every moment.

Those were the dark days of my life, the darkest I have ever faced. They were indeed made all the worse since our great victory over the Blue Korta army that had attacked our mountain fortress. The fact that I had been loath to use our platform death ray projectors on the warships of The Secret Empire of The Hundred Worlds, had seemed such a good strategic plan at the time. Now my lack of aggressiveness had just appeared to open the door for our enemy to take advantage. Zaor said I blamed myself too harshly for all that had transpired, but I could see he was frantic for Manalia's safety even as I was for Sirah's. I realized that my soft Earthly emotions had made me treat the traitors too leniently, my warrior sense of honor was something that villains such as Vakon and Crooch did not possess—and merely saw as weakness. I had been played well by those two treacherous dogs, who counted on me not executing them as soon as they had entered our hidden caves to spew their venomous lies. I was at my wits end.

I sat alone brooding in a dark chamber of our cavern fortress, my head down upon my desk and my thoughts trapped in dark places where I saw no way out. I heard the door open to the room and saw Tor-nul enter. I saw he had someone with him.

Tor-nul bowed, "My Lord, Jon Kirk!"

I lifted my head from the desk in an attempt to show I was in command of my thoughts, but it was a feeble attempt. I was crushed, defeated, all seemed lost then without my beloved Sirah—and yet, as I have always said, I still live. And that is the most important thing of all, for I have always believed that as long as there is life, anything is possible. Even saving Sirah and Manalia.

There had to be a way. I knew I would find it!

"I still live, Tor-nul," I said finding the power within me to raise my voice. Then I repeated to him in a firm tone, "I am a man who has always felt that as long as there is life, anything is possible."

"Yes, My Lord, it is a worthy motto of the warrior code," Tor-nul replied sharply. Then I saw him advance a wily fellow in front of him ushering him forward. This man I recognized as one of the many fellows who had worked with Ras-nor on the death ray weapons.

I looked up boldly, hopefully, gathering myself and speaking with strength as I looked at the newcomer. I remembered him now. "She-fan, it is good to see you again. Have you any news to report?"

I did not expect much at this point, I had him and his rocket men at work for the last few days refitting a ship to take me to the orbiting enemy fleet but all plans were unproductive and to no avail.

"Jon Kirk," She-fan mused, the sadness he felt for my beloved, his Empress, coming through his features and in the tone of his voice, "I am sorry, we cannot build this vessel as you have instructed us to do. We do not have the knowledge. Or at least I do not. Without old Ras-nor to guide us with the ancient knowledge the time limit you gave us will run out."

I sighed. I had expected as much. Time was the key. I was sure that the enemy would keep Sirah and Manalia alive for a time, hostages for the safety of their orbiting warships from our ray projectors, but that would not go on forever. When the usefulness of the hostages ended, that was when I truly feared for their safety. The rub was that I had no idea at all how long the hostages would be kept alive—nor any way to get to the enemy ships to save them.

I silently mused on these dark thoughts when I saw that Tor-nul and She-fan seemed attracted by some commotion down the hall from them in an adjoining cavern. I heard running men, war cries, and growls of anger. I heard the ring of steel upon steel in heated battle. A fight was progressing and nearing my chamber. What now, I though? A rebellion in the ranks? Civil War? An invasion of Blue Kortas? I almost did not care.

Tor-nul immediately called his men together to form a protective ring around me. Tor-nul was not playing, he did not have his men draw their swords, he had them draw their death ray rifles and aim them right at the intruders. As yet he had not given the order to fire, for which I was thankful.

Then I saw the intruders clearly for the first time and I was astonished.

What were these? What were they? In the lead I saw a big burly giant who forced his way into the room through my Black Dragons with another half dozen just like him upon his heels. The intruder and his men did not fight or injure any of my guards, they just quickly and very effectively brushed them aside, but using gestures that did not indicate deadly force. The leader of this band was amazing to look upon, he appeared to be some kind of wild outer space Viking, huge, brutal and fierce. He walked into the chamber like some kind of preternatural force. He was loud and angry. I drew my sword, ready, waiting. If he and his men were some kind of Secret Empire assassins, then I was ready to send them into the Afterworld.

The giant strode before me tall and blustering, his men hulking behind him as Tor-nul's Black Dragons surrounded them all with blasters armed and ready.

"I am Gorm! Gorm of Gorm!" he bellowed simply in a harsh guttural voice as if his name might mean something to me, or any of my people. It did not. But it was not what he said nor his wildness that had Tor-nul, She-fan, myself, along with everyone else in that room staring at him in wonder and utter disbelief—for Gorm was not from Ares at all—Gorm was a non-Ares alien!

Gorm boldly walked over to me with calm intentions, without any apparent menace at all and he certainly showed no fear. I signaled for my men to move back and not to fire their weapons, but they did not lower those weapons. My Black Dragons did not fire and they let him be—for the moment.

Gorm ignoring the weapons trained upon him, said simply, "Are you the one they call Jon Kirk? He who is called the Emperor of the green-skinned people of Ares?"

I nodded. I could see Tor-nul and his men standing ready with drawn death ray weapons trained on Gorm and all his fellows should they make one suspicious move. I motioned Tor-nul once more ordering my commander to hold off on any action for the moment. This strange being interested me. I wanted to hear first what this wild outworlder had to say—and as I myself was an outworlder on Ares—our words would be said one outworlder to another outworlder. I had a hunch that I needed to pursue words with this man.

I looked at him and said boldly, "So you and your companions stole a Secret Empire spy ship and landed here…to spy upon us?" I realized that his ship had not been the small scouting vessel we had noticed after the recent battle where we had defeated the Blue Kortas. The ship that Crooch and Vakon had used to steal away Sirah and Manalia. This was a different spy ship, another ship. Why?

"No, Jon Kirk, what I mean to say is my coming here was no accident. I came here purposefully to seek you out, so we could join our forces with yours and fight The Secret Empire together—Gorms and Ares—as allies."

"Interesting," I answered my visitor thoughtfully, in what I gave in a rather non-committal manner for the moment. I didn't want to seem too eager to join our forces before I knew more about Gorm and these—Gorms? I also did not want to give too much away on what we knew, at least not on the outset. The pain of treachery was still fresh in my mind. I had no idea who this alien creature might be, nor who his people were. I had much to learn first and many questions to ask him, but I was interested in what he had said so far. "How were you able to find me here in the vastness of these Northern Mountains?"

Gorm smiled and just said, "Why, Jon Kirk, I thought you should have guessed that by now. It was through the help of your women, Manalia and Sirah."

Zaor immediately broke ranks and approached the alien rather roughly, "What do you know of Manalia! And The Lady Sirah!"

"Easy, lad!" Gorm warned hotly, but then he cooled down and smiled engagingly, as I noted he took a step back to ward off Zaor's ire. I was sure it was not out of fear, for I was sure the burly space Viking could have done terrible damage to Zaor's lean and trim form had he so desired. But rather, with a dozen death ray pistols trained upon him and his men from Tor-Nul's Black Dragons, he had determined this was not the right place or time to have any kind of battle, even with Zaor's impatient anger.

"Gorm is not here to fight you".

"Gorm, talk to me," I stated firmly, drawing his attention.

Gorm, nodded, motioned for his men to stand back.

"Zaor, hold! Release him now!" Zaor let go of our visitor and moved a few paces back from him. Then looking Gorm squarely in the face I told him, "Gorm, tell me now and truthful, did you in fact see my Lady Sirah, and when did you see her?"

"I did, Jon Kirk, I swear it! We were imprisoned briefly in the cells of the Lord Protector's own warship not long ago. We spoke for a time through a translation device the members of The Secret Empire of The Hundred Worlds have perfected in order to communicate with each other. This device implants the language knowledge of one species into the mind of another so they are allowed to communicate with each other. That is how I am able to come here and to speak to you in words of your very own language."

"She is alive! She is well?" I asked anxiously, trying not to lose control of my emotions, but fairly bursting with joy and a hundred questions now that I knew my beloved Sirah was still alive.

"Well, enough, when I left her, Jon Kirk, I promise you," Gorm stated matter-of-factly. Then with a grimness entering his tone, "At least as well as can be expected after being a prisoner of the Blue Kortas and their Secret Empire masters."

I nodded. At least Sirah was alive! And Manilia too. At least she had been seen alive recently and that thought renewed me, and emboldened me. I knew now what I must do. I looked at the huge wooly barbarian standing in front of me. I said, "Gorm, how many men can fit into that stolen enemy scout flier you came here in?"

Gorm looked at me and smiled, thinking it through, he consulted with his men, then said, "Including myself, no more than six men, but since you Ares men are so small, you may be able to fit nine or ten into the ship."

"And you can fly this vessel, Gorm?"

"Yes, Jon Kirk, I was a slave in the service of The Secret Empire Fleet for years and am able to fly all their vessels. Why?"

"Because, my friend, you and I are going to get into your scout flier and take it to this Lord Protector's ship and rescue my beloved Sirah and Zaor's mate, Manalia, right away!"

Gorm laughed and his men joined in with him, "Jon Kirk, I was wondering when you were going to say that! The Lady Sirah told me you would save her, she told me you would find a way—and if not—that I was to aid you. And I will! I hate the masters of The Secret Empire, I hate their slavery of my people and my world. This offers me and my men a chance to hit them back hard, to hurt them, and we relish the thought. Me and my men are with you, Jon Kirk!"

"I thank you, Gorm," I said, shaking his burly arm.

"I will gladly fly you up to the Lord Protector's vessel, and who knows, perhaps we can do the ships of their fleet some damage along the way!"

"I am sure we can, Gorm," I said with a wry grimace. I was stoked, for now I had what I had needed so desperately, a means to reach the enemy! A means to rescue Sirah! Then I called over Far-nor and told him to prepare all the death ray platform projectors, and that upon a message from me, they are to commence firing at The Secret Empire ships orbiting Ares.

"When you get the word from me, Far-nor, knock them all out of the sky!"

"Yes, My Lord!"

"Zaor, Tor-nul, come on, let's go!"

Gorm led our small party of warriors to his hidden vessel, secreted in a empty cavern at the foothills of the Mountains of Kolver. Our little force consisted of only five men; Gorm; his trusted friend and lieutenant, Tambu; myself; the captain of my bodyguard, To-nul; and of course, Zaor.

"That is a very small vessel," Tor-nul stated with some concern, he was used to the huge wooden ships that traversed the seas of Ares, not this tiny 'flying metal box' of a ship that looked like it was barely big enough to fit the five of us, much less our weapons.

"It will do the trick," Gorm told us with confidence, "of that you can rest assured. Now, all aboard and let us get out of here."

We heeded Gorm's words and soon Gorm, his lieutenant Tambu, myself and trusty Tor-nul and Zaor were all safely belted into seats in the tiny vessel and ready to blast off from the surface of Ares where we would fly through the bright red sky and into the upper planetary atmosphere. The engines of the vessel roared to life under Gorm's control and he checked various dials and gauges preparatory to take off.

"All looks good?" Tor-nul asked a bit nervously, he was unsure of flying and did not like the idea at all of flying machines.

"It will be fine," I answered him.

"Belt yourselves in, this may get a bit bumpy!" Gorm bellowed as he prepared to shoot the tiny vessel upwards into the blood red Ares sky.

"Let's go!" I ordered eager and impatient.

My plan was to somehow link up with and board the warship of the Lord Protector of The Secret Empire of The Hundred Worlds. Once there, I would search for my beloved Sirah, and Zaor for his mate, Manalia. Hopefully we would find both alive and uninjured. Then we would free them and bring them back to the surface of Ares. It was a tall order. A seemingly impossible feat. But I had always maintained that where true love is concerned—the possible is always attainable—the impossible becomes merely probable. I would find Sirah and save her and that was that! And anyone or any *thing* that got in my way was going to find it hard going.

I quickly took out my .45 auto and checked it carefully, then put it snugly into my waist holster. I rechecked the power cartridge on my death ray pistol, saw that it was fully charged, and tucked that into my waist belt on the opposite side from my .45. I then examined my death ray rifle—one of which we each carried with us—just to be sure that it was charged and fully operational and ready for action. For I was sure that we would see action soon and that there would be much blood spilled this day. I only hoped that it would be the blood of our enemies and those who stole Sirah and Manalia away from us.

I also wanted to make sure we rescued the wily old scientist Rasnoor. I needed him back with us, his expertise and knowledge was priceless and key to my plans. I looked around the tiny flier, looking closely at my four comrades: Gorm was busy at the control console of the small craft, growling with impatience as he set and reset dials, he appeared to be very tense and that had me wondering; Tambu sat at his side offering words of encouragement; Tor-nul checked his weapons, and my friend Zaor looked back at me and nodded.

"We will get them back, Jon Kirk," Zaor promised boldly. "I promise it!"

I looked back at my friend. I hoped he was right.

I now noticed that Tambu also carried a captured Blue Korta projectile rifle. I could see that such a weapon could come in handy where we were going. And where we were going was into the maw of the beast, onto an alien enemy interplanetary space warship!

Gorm now started up the rockets and there was a tremendous roar from behind and below us as the giant engines worked their way up to liftoff power.

Gorm said, "Prepare yourselves, takeoff will be instantaneous."

He wasn't kidding either. The roaring grew louder, the tiny craft shook and vibrated and then the sudden jolt shook us wildly before it stopped. Then the movement became smooth and steady. It was almost over before it had begun, and I could now see the bright stars and the blackness of outer space that surrounded us from outside our porthole windows. Now we were flying in outer space. I could see a large red ball of a planet down below us. Ares! So far away!

Gorm sighed, relaxing for the first time in many tense moments, "It is done. We have left the planet and are now in space on our way to Dark Night, the warship that the Lord Protector of The Secret Empire of The Hundred Worlds uses as the flagship of his invasion fleet."

CHAPTER 9

ABOARD DARK NIGHT

Dark Night was truly an enormous warship. I had no idea of the size of the vessel, nor that it was such an incredible vessel, until our tiny scout flier crept slowly towards it. Carefully, slowly we approached. By comparison we were a mere flea upon the body of a mastiff in size. It was an awe inspiring ship.

Gorm spoke up, "See how the damn thing fills the entire forward view screen of our ship. It is immense!"

I nodded, actually awestruck. I began to feel a gnawing fear grow within me that we might just not be up to the task at hand. That thought filled me with fear. I had tried my invisibility device once we got off-planet but it still did not work. I hoped it might work once we were away from Ares and off-planet. It did not. The enemy ships were still jamming the device and their jamming was in effect out here in space as well, as it was upon Ares. It was a grim realization. I now knew that we would have to save the women without using the invisibility device. That was a big blow and it caused my fear to grow for it made the mission much more difficult. Success was probable—I only wondered now if it was actually possible. What if we failed? This was just one of a hundred Secret Empire warships. What did we think we were doing? The enormity of our task really hit me then. What if I never saw Sirah again? What if I was not able to save her? I gritted my teeth and set my jaw firmly with determination to expunge all negative thoughts. Sirah was alive, she was on this ship somewhere, and I would find her and free her if it was the last thing that it did. Since I had come to Ares I had never given up. I would not do so now. I still live! While I lived there was still hope!

Zaor was speechless as he looked upon *Dark Night* while our tiny flier moved around it and came in closer to dock. I could see he was nervous, doubting the success of this venture even as he missed his beloved Manalia. He looked at me and smiled nervously, then said, "It is so big. How can anything be so large?"

"I know," I replied.

"Well, a good friend from a faraway world once told me that as long as there is life, there is hope. I still live, Jon Kirk. You still live! Sirah and Manalia still live! Now all we have to do is go and get them!"

"We can do this, Zaor. We have come this far."

Zaor nodded, "We can do this."

Tambu nodded, but sat with his stoic calm and quiet.

Tor-nul, young and full of energy caressed the hilt of his short sword, ready for action. Upon his lap he held a large death ray rifle which I knew was ready for use. His only hope was that any upcoming battle would be able to be fought and won by the weapons he had, aided by the bravery he possessed in such abundance. I did not want to offer the thought that these vast interstellar warships and space fleets might be something far beyond our scope or powers to deal with. We would see. Soon enough, I knew we would see. I knew how Tor-nul felt, for I felt the same way.

I looked over at the brave captain of my Black Dragons and softly sung the Ares warrior lament that was often spoken or sung before a big battle.

We will do all we can.
A warrior can not do more than that in all honor.
We will do all we can.
For we hold Victory in our hands!

Tor-nul smiled back, singing the Ares reply.

In all honor.
We will do all we can.
We hold Victory in our hands!
That is enough for any warrior!
Victory is ours!

Zaor nodded approvingly.

Gorm and Tambu sat silent in contemplative thought as our tiny vessel approached the loading dock of the huge Secret Empire warship, *Dark Night.*

"I am bringing her in slow. We will dock with them soon, see there…" Gorm said carefully, "the portal opens to allow us entrance."

"Like the whale welcoming Jonah," I muttered.

Zaor looked at me, "I know of no Jo-nah. What do you mean Jon Kirk?"

I looked at him and Tor-nul and put the phrase into Ares terms, "It is like when the great hero, Ry-nar of Ancient Ares walked boldly with sword in hand into the mouth of the terrible monstrous Zarbane, to enter into the beast and retrieve the body of his devoured son, Larl."

Zaor swallowed hard, he was familiar with the dread children's tale. "I think you may be right, Jon Kirk."

Tor-nul just smiled looking boldly at each one of us, "If that is the way it is, then that is the way it shall be. In any case, we are ready."

I smiled back at him, "Spoken like the true fighting man."

"I follow you, Jon Kirk." Tor-nul replied.

Gorm spoke up, "Ready now, we have moved in. We are about to land on the loading dock."

Tambu broke his characteristic stoic silence in dire warning, "We have company. Imperial shock troops, it looks like two full companies of Blue Kortas."

Gorm sighed, picked up his weapon, "Well, comrades, are you ready for a little action?"

"Let's go!" I growled defiantly. "There are enemies to kill and women to rescue. What could be better for any warrior!"

We were now landed and our tiny ship was secured aboard *Dark Night.* Then the doors of our tiny scout ship were suddenly blown open by Gorm and with a wild war cry the five of us charged out into the oncoming waves of Blue Korta shock troops.

They were ready for us of course. The battle was entered into enthusiastically by both sides. The melee was a terrible blow-by-blow battle with swords and daggers—projectile weapons and our death rays—which not only wreaked terrible wounds and damage, but blew holes into walls and men without difference. It caused general bloody chaos among the enemy who were shocked and surprised by the power of our weapons.

I shouted to Gorm who was beside me in the thick of the melee, busy cutting down a Blue Korta, even as I brought down five of the blue beasts with shots from my .45 until it was soon empty. I holstered the empty weapon—I had no time to reload—I brought up my death ray pistol and continued firing, "Quickly, Gorm, leave them for now, lead us to where Sirah and Manalia are held captive."

Gorm dispatched his man with a wild slash, cut the head off another Korta, then moved over to my side just as I blasted one of the enemy who was doing his best to kill Zaor. Zaor quickly nodded his thanks. Then I wheeled to see a huge Blue Korta coming at me with a bloody clever. I raised my weapon, fired—but nothing happened—the power charge in my gun was empty—then I saw a blinding light engulf the Blue Korta just as his clever was mere inches from my head. The enemy warrior just disappeared into a burning incandescent light. Once the light was gone—so was he!

I let out a deep breath and looked to my left to see Tor-nul smiling, patting the stock of his death ray rifle. He had saved my life.

I thanked Tor-nul quickly, picking up another weapon from a fallen Korta soldier and instantly returning fire upon the enemy. Then Gorm and Tambu came over, "Follow us, Jon Kirk, and I shall lead you to your lady."

"Let's go!" I shouted, as exploding projectiles from my weapon found two more of the enemy.

"They are withdrawing!" Zaor shouted hopefully.

"Quick, before they cut us off—Gorm lead the way!"

"Then follow, Jon Kirk, Zaor, Tor-nul, and have a care as we enter the quarters of the enemy."

The corridors of the vast space warship had been sealed and the lights were now off—all was in utter blackness. We were intruders. I knew what the meant. I was sure that the life support on these decks was cut off as well so I knew we didn't have much time to achieve our goal.

"We must make haste, Gorm. they've sealed the decks with an intruder alert and it looks like they've cut off the air supply."

Gorm nodded knowingly, "Follow me."

I was sure that Zaor and Tor-nul didn't have any idea of what I was talking about—they were after all natives of Ares —but Gorm was also an outworlder like myself. As a man of another space faring race, he and his silent companion Tambu understood very well what was happening and knew we had to hurry.

We practically flew through metal encased corridors on that alien ship, many I noticed were lined with rooms or chambers that we ignored. We in kind, were seemingly now ignored by the enemy as well. That was strange. After all, we were invaders here. As we moved further into the ship I noticed that no more groups of warriors met us to bar our path, no snipers harassed our movements, nor attackers entered our path. There were no enemy warriors or inhabitants of this huge ship anywhere we passed, and I began to realize that our path had already been cleared for us. And I began to wonder why.

"It is but a little father. Jon Kirk," Gorm told me.

When we finally reached the end of the long corridor, we found ourselves blocked by a large metal door.

Gorm said, "This is the prison entrance. We have to enter here, it is the only entrance. It opens into a large courtyard—there may be enemies present inside so be ready—count to three and I will blow the door open."

Then I saw Gorm attach a small box-like device to the seam where the two doors met.

"We are ready, Gorm," I shouted. I saw that all my comrades had their weapons drawn and we moved back and tried to cover ourselves.

The explosion was loud and the prison doors blew inward and fell down to clang loudly upon the metal deck floor. It was all so sudden and fast.

When we rushed in I saw what must have been a hundred fully armed Blue Korta warriors baring our path—and worse, out of the crowd of enemies came the arch traitors Vakon and Crooch.

Crooch looked at me and smiled, rubbing his hands together. "Ah, yes, Jon Kirk, so you are here. You have done well to make it this far and my masters are pleased, but you and your comrades will now drop your weapons and submit."

"Never!" I growled my angry defiance, and moved forward ready to attack the mass of warriors determined to sell my life dearly if need be. My companions moved with me, itching for a fight.

Crooch only smiled that oily evil grin of his and I knew that something bad was on its way. "Before you do something foolish, Jon Kirk, take a look above you."

Crooch pointed and I and my companions looked above our heads to a balcony where I saw my beloved Sirah. I yelled with impotent rage, for with my beloved I saw another monster from my past life on Ares, it was none other than my first great enemy, King Tob. Tob, no longer a king now, held my beloved in his huge arms with a dagger to her throat.

"So you see, Jon Kirk," Crooch crooned with his slithering tongue, obviously enjoying his victory over me, "I have the situation well in hand. The woman dies if you and your companions do not drop your weapons immediately."

Gorm looked at me for guidance.

Zaor shouted, "And what of my Manalia!"

Then behind Tob, one of the Blue Kortas brought out Manalia so we could plainly see her also now. She was bound and gagged, and I had to hold Zaor back from rushing to her aid. Zaor raged but I held his sword arm down.

"A valiant but useless gesture, my friend," I told him sadly, "but we still live, and if we live, we may still be of help to our women."

Zaor held back his rage and reluctantly nodded.

Gorm said softly, "I am sorry. We have no choice, Jon Kirk."

I nodded, throwing down my weapons to the floor in disgust. My companions reluctantly did likewise and then we were made captive and led away in chains.

CHAPTER 10

THE PRISON SHIP

We were beaten and chained and then transported to another Secret Empire spaceship, this time a special prison vessel. This ship was enormous and housed thousands of jail cells, some even in artificial habitats —for there were literally thousands of creatures penned there. Some were human, or humanoid, but many were not at all. It was an amazing array of alien life forms from all across the galaxy. We were placed in a cell with three such creatures, and each one of them was an interesting being who I shall give some background on.

The three aliens were Sasheen, a merman sea creature from the water world of Talu; Poln, a *felina* from Caxtar—lately conquered by the warships of the fleet of The Secret Empire of The Hundred Worlds—and lastly; Bran, a space trader from Ko-Ah-Leh, whose people had lately turned to piracy to fight against the ships of The Secret Empire, but now were locked in a war that had become a bloody stalemate. They knew it was just a matter of time before they lost their war and were conquered by The Secret Empire—unless they received help. However, in this part of space, help was in short supply for those in need these days.

Zaor, Tor-nul and myself; along with our alien companions Gorm and Tambu, were now locked in a rather large cell with Sasheen, Poln and Bran. Sasheen had a pool of water in the cell so that the merman could periodically renew his life force and breathing—I was astonished at the fact that the large green and scaly humanoid was able to breath under water and that he also could stay out of water and walk on land for hours at a time. Poln, our *felina* friend was tall and thin, fur covered, with a tiger-like face and coloring. Tor-nul told me that he found her look most attractive. I had trouble getting past the fur in the place of skin, but I assume there was real beauty there. Bran, the space trader from Ko-Ah-Leh was the most colorful, a true rogue, a bandit and pirate at heart—he and Gorm, my huge wild space

Viking-like friend seemed to have much in common and got along well.

The saving grace for me was that Gorm and Tambu spoke the language of all these creatures, called Standard, which he explained to me was the common language of all the planets held under the sway of the Secret Empire of The Hundred Worlds. Thus Sasheen, Poln, Bran and the members of my small party were all able to converse and make ourselves understood. That at least was a positive development. We were all able to speak to each other and we had a lot to talk about. I had a lot of questions to ask them all. What I needed most now was information. Then a plan.

Once we had the introductions over, and learned some of the context of each of our imprisonments—it seemed that like us, Sasheen, Poln and Bran were war chiefs on their respective worlds or leaders of their people against The Secret Empire. Each one in their own way was a leader who fought to resist the dominance of The Secret Empire of The Hundred Worlds on their home planet. They like many imprisoned here represented planets that had once been free. They hated the enemy. I saw they could make good allies.

"So now that we all know each other, and have an equal hatred for this Secret Empire, I say we find a way to break out of here!" I said forcefully, for I was beside myself with apprehension and concern for Sirah. The fact that she was in the clutches of this alien enemy was bad enough, but to see her held captive under the knife of the devilish Tob, and his treacherous allies, Vakon and Crooch, had me almost insane with revenge rage. I knew I had to keep calm, find some way to escape this prison ship—*or to take it!* Then rescue Sirah! In the meantime, if given the opportunity, I planned to wreak as much mayhem and devastation upon the ships of The Secret Empire as possible for what they had done to us.

Zaor was with me, and I know Tor-nul would likewise do all within his power to aid me in rescuing our women and doing all we could to reign havoc upon our enemies. I was also sure of Gorm and Tambu. They were steadfast. So all that was left was to broach the subject of escape and battle with Sahseen, Poln and Bran. I did so with some trepidation, fearing that they might refuse—or worse— that perhaps one of them might be a spy put into our cell to keep tabs on me and my companions. Wily Crooch was not above doing such a thing. But I had to take the chance. I looked at the three non-Ares aliens imprisoned there with us, they seemed honorable and true. I decided that I had no choice but to trust them. After all, they each had their own people to protect and rescue. So I told them I intended to escape.

Bran said it best when he told me, "Jon Kirk, perhaps you have never seen the insides of a Secret Empire prison ship before? I have, numerous times. Believe me, they are not difficult to escape from, but once out of our cell, where do we go? What do we do?"

I nodded, allowing a grim smile to cross my lips, "We will decide that, my friend, once we are free. Right now, there must be some way to escape this cell."

Gorm said, "There is a plan. One that I have been thinking about since they put us in here."

Sasheen spoke up for the first time. "But the being from Ko-Ah-Leh makes sense to me. Once we escape from this cell... Where do we go?"

"We take over this ship!" I said boldly. "It is that simple."

"Take the ship?" Poln said curiously. "I do not know about that. I mean, I am with you, of course, but there are only eight of us."

Bran interjected, "You forget, Poln, Sasheen, that I have been on these prison ships before. We are not alone. We are not the only prisoners here either—and let me assure you—every prisoner on this vessel hates The Secret Empire with a burning passion just as we do. We are not the only prisoners, this vessel is full of thousands of inmates, of all species and races, from over a thousand worlds, and all are potential allies."

"Good, then we break out, and we break them all out too! Then we enlist them all in our cause!" Tor-nul said with hope, speaking up in excitement now that the prospect of action was possible. Action and revenge worked well for Tor-nul.

I looked at my companions, "Yes, we escape and our cause is to destroy The Secret Empire, to take it down from within. Their ships in orbit above Ares are vulnerable."

"Not so fast, Jon Kirk," Gorm added. He was giving me the knowing eye. He knew what I was up to and that it was time for me to show my hand.

"You are correct, Gorm. If we escape this cell we can free all the other prisoners and with their help overwhelm the few Blue Korta guards and then take this ship!"

"You think the other prisoners will fight with us?" Sasheen asked carefully.

Bran growled, "Water-breathing-man, you have no idea the hatred all those imprisoned here feel for The Secret Empire. They will join us, they will fight. Jon Kirk, you have an army in waiting on this ship, now all we have to do is free ourselves and then set them lose. They will join us."

"Then we take the ship?" Tor-nul asked boldly.

"Yes, we take the ship, my friend. But I have an added mission of my own. I must rescue my beloved wife Sirah from the Lord Protector's warship—and Zaor here, must free his beloved mate Manalia from the same incarceration. I know I can count on Zaor and Tor-nul to aid me in this quest, but now I ask you others to aid us also."

Gorm smiled, "I like that, Jon Kirk. Tambu and I are with you. You know you can count on us. Save the women! Death to The Secret Empire! Death to the Blue Korta swine! It is all good."

Then I looked over to Sasheen, Poln and Bran.

"What do you three have to say about that?" I asked them carefully.

Bran just smiled happily, nodded, anticipating action and great adventure with a heavy dose of revenge.

"I am with you too, Jon Kirk," Poln stated simply.

"I may join your quest, but first there is something I need to know," Sasheen asked rubbing the fur of her head carefully. "These women, they are your mates?"

Zaor and I nodded.

"Saving one's mate is a noble quest, Jon Kirk," Sasheen whispered, "it endears one to the gods. I can not refuse such a quest, and if it defeats the minions of The Secret Empire, so much the better. I am with you."

Bran the pirate said carefully, "I know we risk much on your mission, and we will be away from our people for some time. It seems to me we could take this ship, but then it might be wise to go our own way, to escape to another world. However, you want to use the ship to attack the Lord Protector's own vessel. That is a serious move, and something to think about."

"That is so, Bran. I will hold nothing against anyone who will not join me," I stated. I did not expect—could not expect—so many to risk their lives for my own personal cause to save Sirah.

"But there could be great booty in such an action, eh, Jon Kirk? And a captured Secret Empire warship, perhaps afterwards, it can be put into the service of the fleet of Ko-Ah-Leh, perhaps even with one called Bran at the helm?"

I nodded, smiling, "That would be a good use for such a vessel, once it has completed it's mission here."

"You have the soul of a pirate, Jon Kirk. Then I, Bran of Ko-Ah-Leh am with you. We capture this ship and rescue your Lady Sirah and the Lady Manalia. In the meantime we kill Blue Kortas! It all sounds good to me! I am with you!"

CHAPTER 11

THE TAKING OF SOLAR HAPPINESS

Gorm's plan was simple yet effective, and we incorporated into it what Bran knew of The Secret Empire prison ships, in which he had much experience. Thus we had a fairly good idea of what to do and what to expect when I finally gave the word.

We had planned well. In the three days since we had been placed in the cell of this prison ship—which by the way was given the incongruous name *Solar Happiness*—a strangely ironic twist for an incarceration center if ever there was one. Sasheen, Poln and Bran worked well with my companions to achieve that which we all wanted so desperately—our freedom.

I made sure we sounded out other prisoners in nearby cells on their feelings about The Secret Empire. While I did not tell them about my escape plan, I and my companions could easily see these other prisoners would join us in any fight or escape if given the opportunity. They were up for any opportunity to fight their oppressors. It was up to me to make sure they would have that opportunity.

"For freedom, Jon Kirk!" Sasheen replied, "but to a lesser but no less important reason, I desire revenge as well."

I could see Poln and Bran nodding in agreement. Gorm shook his wild mane of long unruly hair, adding, "I like revenge!"

His silent companion, Tambu, just nodded enthusiastically, from where he stood always at the huge Viking-like warrior's side.

"Then we are ready?" Zaor asked quietly.

I nodded, "We are ready", then I gave the signal.

Gorm began it. He lit the fire. We had accumulated paper and scraps from our clothing over the last three days and now had a bundle of flammable material with a fair sized blaze burning in the bunks of our cell.

Sasheen, being a merman from the sea world of Talu was especially fearful of fire, and we all understood his fear. Poln, the *felina*, female tiger-creature, was also fearful of fire, but she stood bravely next to Tor-nul, who tried to comfort her fear. Sasheen lay quietly in his pool of water at the other end of our cell, I could see he was nervous, but he was ready for what would come.

Once the fire was burning well we all shouted in panic for the guards yelling 'fire' for dear life—as we conveniently ignored the water we had access to in abundance in our cell that was in Sasheen's small pool. We just screamed all the louder, starting a panic through-out the entire cell block, and soon other prisoners joined in yelling and shouting, as a small inferno had begun and smoke set off alarms.

"These cells are all monitored with cameras," Bran stated sharply. "The enemy shock troops are on the way and will naturally fear a trap and be ready, nevertheless they are so arrogant and self-confident they believe they can put down any kind of insurrection with ease."

I nodded, the smoke was getting thicker, "All right, it is time."

My order had the desired effect and now as if we were passing out from the thick deadly smoke, we all dropped to the ground and remained motionless. To all effects we were now unconscious or dead from the smoke.

I signaled Gorm.

Then the huge warrior, his aim uncanny, in one fell swoop flung a small hard object at the lens of the camera shattering the glass and rendering it useless to our guards. To all intents and purposes, the fire in our cell was raging and had killed all the prisoners, and the camera had shown that fact to our jailers before the fire had blown I out. Soon the door locks to our cell were put out of working order by the fire as it raged within our cell by the doorway.

Our plan seemed simple enough, but we were on a tight schedule. If the guards did not arrive soon, we would really be dead from the fire—though not the fire actually, but from the smoke inhalation. The smoke was the real danger to us all, except the merman Sasheen. However the fire was his primary danger and it terrified him.

Then the doors were suddenly heard to be unlocked, then broken in as a dozen heavily armed and armored Blue Korta shock troops pushed their way into our cell. The smoke blocked their vision and momentariliary caused them to choke and cough, they immediately switched to air respirators. We all remained motionless upon the floor, where the smoke was less thick and we could still breathe. We hugged the cooler flat metal of the floor silent and motionless for whatever good air we could gasp to keep us alive.

I knew it would not be long now. One way or the other.

I'd told my companions they must be patient. They had to wait. The guards were expecting a sudden attack once they entered our cell, when it did not come, and they saw the raging fire and all the smoke, they were finally convinced this was not an escape attempt. They assumed the fire had killed all the prisoners in the cell. Which is exactly what I wanted them to think. Their over confidence caused them to lower their guard, and that would be their doom.

I counted off the seconds with growing impatience and impending fear, knowing what had to come next. Then the time came.

The Blue Korta officer walked in and looked around, angry and impatient, giving the order that I knew he would have to give. "Sergeant, have your men holster their weapons, put out that dam fire and get these dead vermin out of here now!"

"Yes, commander!" the non-com replied bullying his troops in the typical Blue Korta manner. There was work to do now, no fighting, as they had hoped. "Come on you scum, you heard the commander, put out this fire and get these bodies out of here over to the disposal chute!"

There was mass commotion in the cell. The fire was being put out. Smoke was everywhere. There was movement all around us. All at once we felt the hands of the enemy upon us and we readied ourselves for what was to come. As I had instructed my companions and according to plan, we continued to remain motionless. Playing dead. We held to plan. We were dead weight for the Blue Korta troops as they picked up our bodies. They hated that, and we could hear them complain about picking up our 'dead' bodies. That is just the way I wanted it. To better lift our 'corpses', which were just so much dead weight to them, the guards had to holster their weapons. Some guards even leaned their projectile rifles against the wall of our cell to free their hands to better lift our dead weight, or to drag out our bodies. I dared open my eyes to get a quick look at my surroundings and knew that now was the time to strike. I shouted the code word.

"Freedom!"

Instantly all was confusion, none being more confused than the Blue Korta guards who were completely taken by surprise by our sudden and violent spontaneous resurrection back to life. My companions quickly attacked the enemy with a vengeance. We smashed the totally surprised Blue Kortas, who we had lulled into complete complacency and after knocking them down, we took their weapons.

They had supposed we were all dead from the fire and were loath to begin what they saw as a disagreeable chore. Now each one of my companions was taking down one of the stunned Korta guards in a vicious attack they were unable to fight off.

Now Poln and Bran, Gorm and Tambu, Zaor and Tor-nul and myself were upon the guards knocking them down and out, taking their weapons, and soon shooting them with their own vaulted projectile weapons. Many of the enemy died instantly. Sasheen left his pool and joined us now, wet, but angry and a powerhouse of violence as he took down two surprised Kortas. They could not grasp his slippery merman body, but his massive webbed hands knocked both guards dead with super hard blows. The merman was truly powerful and amazing to see in battle, as were Gorm and Tambu, who with their great size and strength were devastating to the enemy. They were almost the same size of the giant Kortas themselves.

The Blue Kortas were big and deadly fighters, but my companions were equally deadly and what's more, they were full to the bursting point with rage and revenge. They were hungry to fight back after so long being held prisoner. After being so wronged by The Secret Empire. And there was one more thing that I feel created our victory, the realization that we *must* win this battle. We had no choice but to win and escape.

I knew how my companions felt because I felt the same way, my thoughts going to my beloved Sirah, as I pounded one enemy guard after another. I felt that each blow I reigned down upon an enemy took me one step closer to freeing my beloved. I took our enemies' weapons and used them against them as I moved out of the cell into the tight confines of the outer hallway. Cutting our way through their ranks, my warriors forced the Kortas to back off, and we advanced. We put many Blue Kortas to death that day, and with each enemy I and my comrades killed, I felt I was winning closer and closer to taking control of that ship. I needed control of that ship. I knew that I must take the ship if we were to ever really win this battle. It was also the only way that I could reach my beloved Sirah and finally rescue her.

Zaor now returned to my side, just as I dispatched another of the Korta guard with a shot from his own projectile pistol.

"They are all dead, Jon Kirk," Zaor told me with pride. Then he handed me a small group of shiny cut pieces of metal on a metal ring. "These are the keys to this section of the prison. With them we can escape this section of cells and enter other sections of cells and eventually free all the prisoners. We can even reach the control room of the ship."

"Good! Let's do it!"

Soon we had other sections of the ship that held cells opened and we released the prisoners. We rushed to the outer hallway, meeting only token resistance now. It seemed that the ruckus we had begun in the prison ship had spread and become a general and total chaos throughout the entire vessel. The prisoners were all set free, and they wasted not one second joining in our fight against their guards.

Soon the token resistance of the last few Blue Korta guards ended with their death and our tiny band of warriors ran to the outer locks that would give us entrance into the main hallway of the mighty vessel, and eventually, all other sections of the prison ship—including the control room.

"Gorm, you take some men, make sure all the prisoners are freed and have them pledge themselves to our cause," I ordered sharply.

Gorm nodded, left immediately on his mission with Tambu at his side

Then I quickly took Bran aside, "You know these larger ships well, take me to the bridge—or whatever works here as a control room. We're going to take control of this ship and I want to get to the captain and his people right away, before they realize the full extent of what has happened here. They have lost the day, but I do not want them to do anything drastic, like flooding the decks with poison gas."

Bran swallowed nervously, it was evident he had not thought of that, then he added fearfully, "Or something really stupid, like self-destruct the ship."

I winced, now I hadn't thought of that. It hadn't occurred to me that the enemy might go that far to stop us, but perhaps… It just made it all that much more imperative that Bran and I reached the bridge and neutralized the captain and his crew right away before they could alert the other ships of the fleet. For they did that, the fleet would blow this ship out of space once they discovered what had happened here.

"Come on, let's go! We have to reach the bridge before they blow the ship!" I shouted.

Then I saw Gorm moving down the hallways as Bran led me down another hallway and then up an elevated tube to the captain's bridge.

Solar Happiness was anything but a happy ship just then. And the captain, a gruff old Blue Korta with a crew made up of Zaran

Winged-men and a race of beings who were called Tergats—tall gangly humanoids with yellow skin and elaborate upper body fins—were his bridge crew.

Bran and I burst into the bridge with a stupendous bang, each of us dropping a Winged-man and Blue Korta trooper, then another each of the crew, just to get their attention and let them know we were there and serious.

The captain turned on us fuming, cursing, screaming orders to his crew, "Kill them! Kill these intruders!"

No one moved.

Bran and I had our rifles trained on them all and they knew that if even one of them made so much as a move we would drop him without a thought. The crew made signs of peace and surrender and Bran barked orders to them to drop all weapons and not to make a move.

"We have your ship, Captain."

"You do not! Kill them!" he barked enraged.

Not one of the crew moved a muscle. I could see Bran's trigger finger moving with itchy anticipation.

"If you do not surrender, you will die," I barked back, pointing my projectile rifle directly at him in case he had not seen it before. "I have no time to play games with you, Captain."

"I will never surrender!" he shouted and suddenly he drew his sidearm and raised it to fire.

I was expecting such a foolish gesture of course, and quickly cut him down with my own projectile rifle. He died quickly, but painfully, his cries of pain filled the bridge for many seconds before he expired, his ghastly death causing his crew to soften their resolve against us substantially.

I looked at the rest of the bridge crew, "If you do not surrender and follow my orders, then you die." I said matter-of-factly, which I could see after the death of their captain, had a much more powerful effect upon each one of them.

However, one bold fellow, one of the Tergats, pulled a weapon that he must have had secreted upon his person. Bran saw the move in a flash and hit him squarely in the head with a shot, and the Tergat fell forward onto the metal floor in a bloody mess that all there were started to view.

"Anyone else?" I asked, my voice full of deadly menace.

There was utter silence in reply.

I nodded, "that is better."

The bridge crew said nothing, but remained frozen in fear.

Then I heard it, footsteps running toward the bridge from the outer hall. Bran and I looked at each other in alarm. I said, "You watch the bridge crew, I'll take care of our visitors."

Bran nodded. We stood back to back. I aimed my weapon to the door ready to fire and destroy anyone who came through that door.

Suddenly the door opened, I heard my name spoken, "Jon Kirk!"

"Tor-nul!" I barked quickly.

"Yes, it is I," he said with an easy smile. "Jon Kirk it is good to see you, and you as well, Bran. And I see that you have captured the control room crew."

I nodded, he looked over at the body of the captain, his braid uniform indicating his rank, and added, "But I see the captain did not make it."

"He proved to be a most uncooperative fellow," Bran replied with a knowing leer.

"And what of the prisoners in the inner cells?" I asked.

Tor-nul grinned enthuastically, "They are all set free and all have joined with us Jon Kirk. The ship is ours!"

"The ship is ours!" I shouted.

Bran let out a loud whooping holler.

I looked over to the control room crew of *Solar Happiness*. I told the crew, "If you pilot the ship for us and do not give us any trouble you can live, and you have my word we will set you free once we are done. Of course if you refuse, or cause trouble…" I made a motion to their dead captain laying in a pool of blood at my feet. "What do you say?"

Tor-nul added so all could hear, "Jon Kirk, we do not need these people now. There are many prisoners we have released who can fly this ship. We should have all the enemy crew remaining put to death immediately."

I smiled, I knew what my lieutenant was doing, putting on a bit of a show for the bridge crew. It could not help but be effective.

Tor-nul's harsh words had caused great consternation among the crew, who had been fearful before, but now where positively frantic. They spoke rapidly among themselves.

Of course that did it! A tall Tergat, taller even than his tall fellows, who identified himself as Sharn, a lieutenant of the fleet and Sub-commander of *Solar Happiness* prison ship now spoke up. "We will do as you require. We do not want to die. We are all *consignats* here…"

I looked over at Bran for an explanation of the word which I had not heard before.

"*Consignats* are… They have been forced into military indenture by their masters to serve The Secret Empire. This is how the empire fill the ranks of their army and how they crew their massive warships. Only the captain and his chief military aides, along with some Blue Korta bodyguards, are regular Empire troops."

I looked at Sharn and Bran with many ideas brewing. I saw Sharn nod his head to me in agreement with what Bran had said. If that was true this vaulted Secret Empire was actually a vast slave empire with little loyalty by its members, and I was now determined to bring it down.

Bran continued, "I was a *consignat* once… It is not… I think these people will not go against us, Jon Kirk. Their hearts are just not in it. They only serve because they are forced to do so."

I looked at the Tergat named Sharn, and the rest of his people who were the only ones remaining of the enemy force in the control room. The captain, and all Winged-men and Blue Kortas long since having died in battle.

"Very well, Sharn, you and your people will pilot the ship. It is my ship now. Do you understand?"

"Yes, My Lord," Sharn replied.

"Good. Now after we take the Lord Protector's ship—"

"Take the Lord Protector's ship!" Sharn gasped in alarm.

"Fear not, we have a plan. It can not fail. Then, after we take his ship, you will pilot Bran back to Ko-Ah-Leh and then you and your other Tergats are free to return to your own world in peace."

Sharn nodded thoughtfully, talking it over quickly with his companions.

"I suppose that is acceptable, it seems that we have little choice in any event," Sharn said quietly, still thinking it through. It was a bit more than he and his people had signed on for. Agreeing to join us and pilot the ship for our escape was one thing—fighting the flagship of The Secret Empire fleet—and their fleet of warships—was quite another. There were almost a hundred ships orbiting Ares with the flagship.

Bran patted the stock of his projectile rifle, and looked intently at the Tergat, "Brother, one always has a choice, all that is needed is for the truly wise man to make the *correct* choice. You can not go wrong if you follow Jon Kirk and join his cause. He seeks to destroy The Secret Empire. I would think it is something you and your Tergats would approve of heartily."

"We do, we do, but…" Sharn replied softly, looking at me carefully. "I admit, we are fearful. We are pilots and not warriors. It seems to be a massive and dangerous undertaking."

"You are correct, Sharn," I told the tall Tergat truthfully, "But if you and your people join us willingly, fight beside us, you also fight for yourselves and your freedom. To free your Tergat world."

Sharn nodded, "Then Jon Kirk, we are with you. I await your orders."

"Good," I said, relieved that the Tergats seemed to be with us now fully. I had no desire to imprison them, nor fight against them. "Sharn, you are ship's captain now, set a course for the heart of The Secret Empire fleet and bring us up to the Lord Protector's flagship. Make sure no warning of what has transpired here gets through to anyone in the enemy fleet."

Sharn saluted briskly and then gave his fellow Tergats orders to accomplish my wishes.

I turned to Bran and Tor-nul. "Well, my friends, we have a lot of work to do before we dock with the Lord Protector's ship. Are you ready?"

"Ready as ever!" Bran and Tor-nul shouted together.

CHAPTER 12

LORD PROTECTOR DOOM

Lord Protector Karlath Doom of The Secret Empire of The Hundred Worlds warship watched through the screen with interest as the prison ship *Solar Happiness* moved closer to perform a docking maneuver with his own fleet flagship, *Dark Night*.

"So, Quarto?" Doom growled in utter annoyance to the captain of his warship, "What does the captain of *Solar Happiness* want to tell me that is so important that it necessitates he take his ship off station and come here so he can personally speak with me?"

Quarto saluted briskly, bowed his head. "He says it is secret, My Lord. For your ears only. He says that it is valuable information he took from a prisoner who has news of the enemy fleet that has been sent against us."

"Hah!" Lord Doom growled with disdain. "He had better be correct, or his head will decorate the prow of this ship!"

Captain Quarto swallowed nervously and bowed once again. While he was a ferocious Winged-man and captain of a warship in his own right—this after all, was Lord Protector Doom himself. Doom was a man of great and potent powers, and not all of them said to emanate from the natural world. For Lord Protector Karlath Doom was a Sindaki—from that dark, faraway word where it is said the inhabitants could delve deep into the minds of various races and take control of their wills. Such was the theory of how The Secret Empire of The Hundred Worlds had originally achieved their dominance over dozens of races and hundreds of planets throughout known space.

Captain Quarto—a Winged-man himself from Zar—was one who while having family on Ares had never in his life been to that world they were in orbit around now. He had never seen Lord Doom use his terrible powers on anyone and he hoped that he never would. Quarto for a Winged-man—though one from the home world of Zar—might be said to be somewhat more civilized than his Ares counterparts, who recently had been routed on that world by the green-skin humans. Quarto was also a *Shorns*, a member of a religious sect on Zar who believed in peace and was against violence. *Shorns* also did not eat meat, any form of meat, and they made very knowledgeable ship's officers.

"That prison ship captain had better have something worthwhile to report to me, or it shall be the last report he ever makes," Doom growled, watching the two ships come closer together preparing to dock. "Quarto, tell me again what news or information he said he was bringing?"

Quarto swallowed tightly, shifted his command console so that his wings—folded back now in the reclined 'Nee-position—would be more comfortable and said, "Great Lord Protector, the captain said he has tortured and broken some outworlder prisoners and that they have valuable information for the empire."

"Be more specific, Quarto!"

Quarto swallowed hard, "My Lord, the prison ship captain refused to offer specifics over open space communications channels for security reasons."

Doom nodded, annoyed but acknowledging the need for security in such a sensitive matter. It had just better be worth it!

"They approach, Master," Quarto stated, waiting. Then he said, "And now… Good, they are docked."

The Lord Protector nodded impatiently.

Captain Quarto turned to his subordinates barking orders, "Nem-ha, stabilize trajectories and lock rotation. Asur, you may begin pressurization of airlock. Trashur, have a contingent of Blue Korta shock troops meet the captain and bring him here immediately. Lord Protector Doom is waiting!"

Acknowledgement of Quarto's orders was instantaneous and automatic.

"Lord Doom?" Captain Quarto asked, noticing his master was looking at him intently. Carefully. That look always made the captain very nervous. It was almost like he could speak, without having to use words, to make his desires known, or his intentions understood, by the mere power emanating from his coal black eyes.

"We are losing precious time, Captain. The enemy fleet will be in position for their initial attack soon. The Enemy Empire has fought us long and hard here at this strategic area in the galactic core—which encompasses this troublesome Ares system. We have done well, fought well, but our empire is no match for theirs. It will not allow another defeat. Let us hope this prison ship captain brings us good news. I have a feeling within me that something big is going to happen here, a massive change is coming, perhaps it is the great victory we seek? We may use this news once and for all to destroy our enemies."

Quarto nodded. He was one of the privileged fleet officers of The Secret Empire of The Hundred Worlds—and in charge of the flagship of the Lord Protector's fleet. He knew the true politics of the Hundred Worlds and the death-battle his empire was in with the hated and anti-humanoid Enemy Empire. It had become a strange and vicious political and military struggle with some mysterious alien entity that was known by many names: sometimes called the Emperor of The Known Universe—the Kin-Ty-Roo—or He Who Is Not To Be Named. By any name the alien entity put fear into the hearts of all alike, Winged-men from Zar, powerful Sindalki lords, all Secret Empire minions.

When The Secret Empire of The Hundred Worlds had first encountered the empire of the Kin-Ty-Roo a hundred years ago, their warships had won a stunning battle—destroying what turned out to be not some massive war fleet, but in reality was just a small exploratory force. The stunning encounter had caused the leadership of both empires to reel in shock and fear at the existence of the other. Little did either empire realize at the time that they had unleashed a torrent of vicious creatures in war against each other, some of whom were so alien, so brutal, and so persistent in their cunning warfare that all the violence and arrogance of the empire Quarto served could not stop the superior and unending onslaught of this new enemy.

"They are not like us at all, Lord Protector," Captain Quarto spoke up, uncharacteristically speaking directly to his master unheeded. "We are different as well, yet each race in our empire has similar characterizes, humanoid shape of some kind, basics of appearance such as one head, two or four upper appendages, wings or scales, sexual reproduction. They are unlike us, even the strangest of us. They are truly amorphous, of shifting form and indistinct substance, totally alien so that we can not even communicate nor comprehend them."

"You seem to know much about them, Captain." Doom observed critically.

Captain Quarto grew nervous, he was not used to speaking up, and never directy to a Sindalki lord, "My Lord, I study them, I try to learn about them. What little I can. It is a hobby of mine."

"Hobby? Perhaps you should take up another hobby before this one does you ill?" Doom snarled.

"Yes, My Lord, of course!"

"You are all wrong about them, you know," Doom said sharply.

"Yes, My Lord." Quarto answered in astonishment, but he knew that his Sindalki lord must know the real truth. While he was bursting with questions, he did not think it wise to ask his lord them at this time.

Doom smiled evilly, and for a moment Quarto felt as if the Lord Protector had somehow entered his mind. How had he done it? What was he looking for? Then the connection was broken as quickly as it had been made. Quarto sighed deeply as cold sweat ran down his dark leathery face.

Doom spoke once more, "We can comprehend one thing and that is all we need to comprehend, Captain, the hate they extrude to us is matched only by the hate we feel toward them."

Quarto nodded, as it was not a good thing to disagree with Lord Protector Doom on any matter, but he was skeptical of his master's words all the same. Finally his train of thought was broken by an announcement from one of his officers, Lieutenant Nemha.

"Captain Quarto," Nemha chimed, "I am to report that the captain of *Solar Happiness* and his routine await in the next chamber."

Quarto nodded, spoke curtly to another bridge officer, "Scan them, Asur."

Asur looked into a screen, counted what appeared to be two dozen shock troops surrounding an indeterminate amount of visitors.

"All looks as it should be, My Captain," Asur replied briskly.

"Then pass then in, Asur. Hurry now, Lord Protector Doom awaits!"

* * * *

I wanted Gorm to be the first of our party to enter the bridge of *Dark Night*—dressed as he was as a Blue Korta shock troop officer—with Tambu at his side similarly attired, the two monsters strode into the room like they owned it. The two giants fit in well to those who saw them at first glance. They were just as they appeared to be, they were good enough deceivers to allow my band to follow quickly behind them onto the bridge of the Lord Protector's own flagship. We strode in boldly, all eyes upon us, there were salutes but there was no suspicion yet. We were in!

Meanwhile I knew that in the rest of the ship, the battle for control had already begun. With the two ships docked now, all hell had broken lose fast and furious as the former prisoners and slaves from *Solar Happiness* invaded *Dark Night* and took a mighty toll on the enemy. A mighty battle was waged below decks for control.

Our new death ray rifles made quick work of the totally surprised Blue Korta troops, who using mere projectile weapons were hit very hard and took many losses. They soon discovered they were hopelessly outclassed with their next-to-useless and now obsolete projectile weapons versus our more deadly death ray guns. The fight was short and furious but the battle was over literally before the enemy ever knew what hit them.

Immediately hundreds of former prisoners who had now become free fighters for our cause were itching for revenge—and they took it out upon their former guards with relish. When the deed was done, they collected the uniforms and weapons off the enemy dead and those who surrendered. Then those of our men that fit into the uniforms, took the place of the Blue Korta shock troops. In most cases, a quick look at our men in the enemy uniforms would not give away the deception right away. That hesitation was all it took, that was all our men needed.

The change of uniforms had not make a perfect match for my own group but I chose warriors who in a pinch it would work well enough to get me and my companions into the enemy ship and up to the bridge where the Lord Protector held sway.

When the doors were opened upon Lieutenant Asur's order, we were ready.

Lord protector Doom came into the room with Captain Quarto. The two leaders were in deep conversation and did not notice us right away. My men fanned out, quickly and silently they took out the guards.

Finally the Lord Protector took one look at us and realized what was up, he shouted almost at once, "It is a trick! Kill them all! Kill them all now!"

By that time he was too late, the battle for the bridge had already begun and would soon be over.

With Gorm and Tambu in the lead, myself and a dozen weary but vengeful warriors stormed into the bridge. By my side was my good friend Zaor and faithful Tor-nul. Accompanying us was Poln, the *felina*. She fought with claws and fangs, ripping and tearing into the enemy like a female tiger demon, forcing the enemy away from her in terror. Sasheen the merman, and Bran the pirate joined us bringing with them a good assortment of armed prisoners we had liberated from *Solar Happiness*. All were hungry for battle.

The entire scene instantly became a shambles as weapons were fired in every direction and fighters began falling on both sides in a vicious conflict in what now seemed like a cramped bridge. This area was never intended for such close quarters fighting—nor with use of death ray blaster weapons—where every shot that missed or went wide meant a control console was damaged or set afire. Or walls and bulkheads were perforated. These were thankfully quickly patched up by the warship's own automatic defense system and shields.

"Over here!" I shouted to Zaor and the others. Now I moved in on the Lord Protector himself, firing my blaster at his few defenders as I approached him. He had been hiding behind a ring of his officers, each of whom was fighting furiously as we advanced, laying down their own lives for their master.

"Surrender!" I demanded.

"Never!" one of the officers who I assumed to be the captain of the guard replied in defiance.

"No need to die for nothing," I barked. "Surrender and you will be fairly treated."

In answer, their leader ordered his defenders to fight harder. They were brave and very foolish. I realized that these men feared their so-called Lord Protector more than they did me and my vengeful escaped prisoners. That told me something about our enemies. Meanwhile, the fight raged on. Shots were fired, bodies fell, men yelled out in pain from terrible wounds. However, their defense was to no avail, the die was already cast, and my men finally mowed down the last few defenders. Only the ship's captain and the Lord Protector were left alive.

The Captain dropped his weapon, and the Lord Protector did not seem armed, so I was sure we had them now. Then the Lord Protector took me by surprise by grabbing his own ship's captain in a half-nelson kind of hold and shoving the barrel of a small hand blaster he had suddenly taken from the folds of his robes, against his own captain's head. The Captain—I recognized him immediately as one of those Zaran Winged-men who had never been native to Ares—stood by as perplexed and hopeless as us all by his master's sudden and inexplicable action.

"Hold your fire!" I shouted to my men. I knew that many of them were taken aback by the sudden turnabout and had itchy trigger fingers. Most would just as soon kill both of these enemies as soon as possible, but I wanted them to hold off for the moment. Then to our enemy holding the captain I asked, "You are the Lord Protector?"

"Lord Protector Doom, to you, creature!" he barked back.

I smiled at this insult, then I firmly ordered him, "Put your weapon down. You have nothing to fear from us if you surrender. You will be treated fairly. Save yourself and your brave captain."

Then Lord Protector Doom shocked us all—he must have used some of the ancient Sindaki magic he and those of his exalted status were known for—for suddenly he dropped the ray gun—quickly spun around in a blinding whirlwind of bright light—and then immediately disappeared!

Just like that he was *gone!*

I was stunned. We were all stunned.

Doom had been there one moment—gone the next.

I immediately wondered if it had been some trick of invisibility—then remembered how the Blue Kortas and The Secret Empire ships on Ares had been able to jam our own invisibility devices making them useless. So his action was probably not simple invisibility—it was probably something much more. But what? Regardless, I still had to make sure he was not merely invisible now, so I had to find out what I could about what he had just done. I could not allow Doom to escape. So I quickly drew my sword and slashed the empty air where he had been standing just a split second before. Zaor and Tor-nul did the same. Between us we three covered the entire area the Lord Protector might have been hiding if he was actually invisible. Our sword blades hit nothing at all. He was not invisible. He was simply gone. I wondered how he had been able to disappear like that, and where he had gone to?

The captain, as big a Winged-men as I had ever faced before, growled in anger at what had been done to him by his leader.

"Where did he go?" Gorm barked.

"Did you see that?" Bran shouted perplexed.

"What happened, Jon Kirk?" Tor-nul asked, suspicion making way to fear. "He just—just disappeared into thin air before our eyes!"

"They are devils!" Gorm growled, "I have heard tell of this Sindaki magic. Wily cunning devils, and that Sindaki lord has mysterious powers. I am sure he is watching us at this very moment from whatever dimension of nether space he has entered."

We all looked around nervously.

Gorm's words caused me to think about what had happened with an Earthly explanation. But his words caused everyone to turn around suspiciously, nervously leveling blasters in all directions. However, there was nothing there to see, only the carnage of the recent battle, the dead men who had been the officers and crew of *Dark Night*. Nothing more.

No Lord Doom.

Then an alarm shrilled.

I looked to the Zaran, the ship's captain, who had not resisted and was being held fast by our men. He was looking around himself, and at us, in astonishment.

"What does that alarm mean, Captain?" I asked harshly, fearful of what he might tell me.

Still stunned, shocked, the Zaran could not believe we had taken his ship—The Lord Protector's own ship! I had Zaor and Sasheen bring him closer to me.

"You are our prisoner, but if you work with us you will not be harmed and when this war is over you will be released," I told him bluntly but truthfully.

He appeared to be thinking it over, nodded acknowledging defeat finally, then said, "You are the one called Jon Kirk? The leader who routed my people from Ares. I hope you realize that not all Zarans are as corrupt and decadent as those Winged-men who occupied the surface of your world. We *Shorns* are not like them at all."

I did not know exactly what he meant by that but I found that hard to believe, knowing the Winged-men as I did, having so much interaction with them upon Ares. Could some of them actually be different? *Shorns*? What were they? I seriously doubted it, but I was interested in what this one had to say.

"Yes, I am the one known as Jon Kirk."

"For myself, I want nothing but to return to my beloved planet Zar. To fly once again through the azure skies of my home world in peace. I and all those on this vessel in the service of the Lord Protector are *consignats*…"

"I am familiar with the term," I told him.

He nodded, keeping his wings folded behind him, as Zaor kept a weapon trained upon him. "Then you understand how it is with us?"

"Perhaps, but I have been tricked before, and I have limited patience and less mercy for liars and scoundrels," I told him truthfully.

"Yes, I understand. I will cooperate with you, Jon Kirk," the Zaran told me flat out. I was rather astonished by his sudden change of sides, he certainly didn't seem to be like any Zaran I had ever encountered before. Was this another trick? Or was he just a practicable creature? And where had Doom disappeared to?

"Good, then tell me where Lord Doom is?" I asked sharply.

The Zaran bowed, "I do not know, that is the truth, he is gone. Just gone. They—the Sindaki—He has…powers."

I wasn't sure if he was being truthful or not, but when dealing with a Winged-man it is always best to assume the worst. Assume the worst but I knew this one could prove useful. "What is your name?"

"I am called Quarto, captain of this vessel *Dark Night*, flagship of Lord Protector Karslath Doom, a master of The Secret Empire of The Hundred Worlds—and I am at your service, Jon Kirk."

I looked at him sharply, in almost absolute disbelief.

Captain Quarto bowed slightly, formally.

I looked at him again, returned his bow, asking, "And what of Lord Doom? Where has he gone?"

Captain Quarto thought this over carefully, shrugged his huge winged shoulders, then said, "A mystery for certain, My Lord. He is one of the Sindaki and they are strange and have magical powers. They are the controllers of the Hundred Worlds, of The Secret Empire, of us all. I do not know much about him. Lord Protector Doom is not in the habit of confiding in underlings and in those he considers to be lesser beings."

I nodded and stored that information for the moment. Of course we checked the room for some kind of secret door or hidden room, compartment, or corridor for his escape, but there was nothing. It really did appear as if he had just disappeared—or I realized—he had somehow dematerialized his body and left the ship—or at least the bridge.

I put Lord Doom's whereabouts on hold for the moment to concentrate on that alarm blaring throughout the bridge—I was also chaffing at the bit to save Sirah and Manalia. Then I realized what the alarm was for.

"Orbital decay, you said, Captain?" I asked him quickly. "Can you correct it?"

Captain Quarto smiled with grim pointed Winged-men teeth, "Of course. It is a relatively minor correction—not serious as long as it is not left unattended for too long a time. Should I correct the orbit now?"

"Then, yes please, Captain, you may correct the orbit and then run your vessel normally. My men Gorm and Tambu and these others will assist you."

Gorm and Tambu shrugged unenthusiastically, they would have far better liked to kill the Winged-man captain, than work for him. But I insisted. Captain Quarto spoke quickly to my men and assigned each a station on the bridge and told them what to do.

Gorm sat down at the navigator's console, after unceremoniously removing the dead body of the former occupant of that station.

Tambu did likewise at the helm.

I motioned Sasheen to monitor communications and let us know if anything unusual was coming over the com link. So far, it looked like the rest of the fleet did not know about the battle on the bridge and the capture of the Lord Protector's ship or the prison ship. I knew the situation would not remain that way for long.

Captain Quarto seemed to have stood by his word to me and he kept everything operating under normal fleet procedures. I wondered how he dealt with the situation when another captain in the fleet wanted to speak to the Lord Protector personally, but I assumed Quarto was more than able to stall the other captains for a bit. If Secret Empire standard operating procedures were in use throughout the fleet, I knew it would be a very bold captain indeed who sought to override Quarto if he told them the Lord Protector was busy and did not want to be disturbed. No captain under those circumstances would demand to speak to Lord Protector Doom. That said, I wondered just where Doom had disappeared to? It did not seem that he was on another warship in the fleet, for I was sure we would have heard about that right away as he mobilized the rest of the fleet against us. I was sure there would have been rapid heavy weapons fire against our ship and eventually storming Blue Korta boarders. I wondered just where that demon cur had gone and what his game was.

Captain Quarto proved as good as his word. He corrected the orbital decay and stabilized the orbit of the ship. The alarm soon died away. I sighed in relief. The lack of that searing sound replaced by quiet was a real blessing. The ship appeared to be functioning normally and Quarto was running things as if Lord Protector Doom was still in charge and on his flagship. But where was Doom?

I had Gorm use the monitors to run a detailed scan throughout the ship for Lord Doom, or any Blue Korta warriors or enemy troops that may have been missed in our takeover. I was sure there might be an occasional straggler hiding out, ready to make mischief. I was also sure Lord Protector Doom was planning mayhem and murder, but as yet he had not made his plan known nor shown any reappearance. That had me stumped, and fearfully nervous, for I knew the other shoe had to drop sometime soon. I was worried that the longer it took for Doom to make his presence known, the worse it would be for us all. What was he up to?

Once Gorm completed the scan, he told me, "Good news, Jon Kirk, the entire ship has only ten enemy crewmen left—they are in the engine room and accompanying battery—but they are under direct orders of Captain Quarto who controls them. They are also *consignats*, so they have all agreed to join us and cooperate. There do not seem to be any living Blue Korta troops onboard. We terminated them all after we docked and took the ship."

I nodded. That was good news, at least, but I still worried about Doom.

I asked Captain Quarto, "There is a prison area on this vessel where important prisoners are kept. One of them is my beloved wife and Empress Sirah—the other is Zaor's mate—Manalia. Do you know where these women prisoners are being kept in this vessel? My man Gorm tried to find the place, but was unable."

Captain Quarto nodded, "These are what are called strategic prisoners."

"Political prisoners," I corrected, offering the true term for them.

"Yes. Doom had the location of the cells changed after Gorm and Tambu escaped. Jon Kirk, I will have all such political prisoners released and brought here immediately. Do not fear, my men are all loyal—to *me*. They will do as *I* say—and I will do as *you* say—at least for the present."

I nodded, I could not ask for more than that of a Winged-man. "Good, Captain. Now have my wife, Sirah, brought to me here. Please."

Captain Quarto gave the commands and in a short time Sirah and I were holding each other tightly within our arms upon the ship's bridge. Manalia and Zaor were also together again much to their joy.

"I knew you would come, My Emperor!" Sirah cried, tears streaming down her face. Our long separation was at long last finally over, but we were still not out of danger.

"Are you well?" I whispered as we smothered each other with kisses. "You are Uninjured?"

"Yes, and you?" she asked softly stroking my arm.

"I am fine, now that we are reunited," I told her as I ran my fingers through her lush green hair and held her closer to me. I never wanted to let her go again. I saw that Zaor and Manalia were together at last and I was happy for them.

"Oh, Jon," Sirah cried, "I am so happy. I knew if anyone could save me it would be you. But how did you accomplish such a feat? I feared you would not get my message. And is little Alun safe?"

"I will explain all later, my beloved, but for now we are together, however the danger is not over. And yes, our son is safe and back in the caves on Ares with a hundred Black Dragons to protect him and nurses to provide for his every need. Fear not."

"I do not fear now, My Lord, Emperor," she said with a little smile. "But whatever is to come, at least we shall face it together."

I smiled back, "Yes, we shall face it together. To victory!"

"To victory!" Sirah replied boldly.

"We did it, Jon Kirk!" Zaor shouted to me in wild excitement from where he was holding Manalia once again in his loving arms. "We saved them! You saved them!"

I was about to reply when our ship was suddenly rocked back and forth from what seemed to be a terrific explosion.

I shot a rapid-fire look at a very surprised Captain Quarto.

"What is it!" I barked.

Quarto looked grim, then shouted, "We are under attack, My Lord! The war fleet of the Enemy Empire has arrived and is doing battle with the fleet of The Secret Empire of The Hundred Worlds! The enemy warships are here to destroy our fleet!"

I nodded, it did not surprise me, from the frying pan into the fire, I thought.

CHAPTER 13

THE ENEMY EMPIRE ATTACKS!

"Captain Quarto, you have to coordinate our defense—and then get us out of here!" I ordered the large winged creature who ran the Lord Protector's flagship.

"Impossible, My Lord, we have almost a hundred warships in this area—all warships of the fleet that have been waiting for so long to do battle with the fleet of the Enemy Empire. We must fight! I must direct our defense and then attack!"

Then Captain Quarto gave orders for the prisoner vessel *Solar Happiness*—which was still docked to his warship—to be cut lose immediately.

No sooner had the ship been detached then it was hit with a torrent of incoming enemy fire. Unmanned now, a useless derelict in space, without shields raised, it was cut to pieces by enemy fire and moments later exploded in a blast of bright incandescent light.

"What are you going to do, Captain?" I asked concerned as I held Sirah in my arms while our ship was buffeted with enemy blasts. Luckily our shields held firm. While my sword arm was ready and willing for any fight that might come up—and our ray rifles were powerful weapons—I knew that this type of ship-to-ship space warfare far outclassed any of our puny individual weapons. It was almost enough to dampen the spirit of any fighting man, but I would not hear of it, and Captain Quarto seemed well in command and was ready to direct his fleet to fight. I knew that at this point there was only one thing for us to do—fight and win—or be destroyed! As captain of The Secret Empire flagship, Quarto saw to it that orders of battle were sent to his ships and ordered his captains on a plan to engage the enemy and defeat them. The Captain told all of us to strap in and to man the various projectile weapon batteries of his huge warship.

"Are you ready, Jon Kirk? Ready Aresans, Gorms, Telgars!" Quarto growled, while he continually barked out commands to Gorm at the navigation station and Tambu at helm. "We are moving off. Once we regroup the fleet I will lead them in an attack. Sasheen, patch through a communication link to all Secret Empire ships—captain to captain."

Sasheen the merman seated at the com link set up the connection immediately.

Soon Sasheen cut in, "Captain Quarto, the link is established."

"Fine, Sasheen," the captain replied. Then he spoke in a loud and powerful tone. "Comrade captains of the glorious fleet of The Secret Empire of The Hundred Worlds, Lord Protector Doom has… been called away, and I, Captain Quarto have assumed command of the flagship *Dark Night*, and of our fleet. Prepare to do battle with this fleet of the upstart virus that we call the Enemy Empire and the alien entity that so arrogantly calls itself the Emperor of the Known Universe. We will see about that, my brother captains! Upon my order, form pattern BZ24 with Captain Hotath's group to outflank the attackers on the right. Command order, Quarto, captain Secret Empire fleet, so ordered, this date, out."

Quarto sat down in the command console. For a Winged-men from Zar he had done an outstanding job, his performance seemed to have worked. I knew that being under attack, The Secret Empire fleet had to fight, defend itself, and hopefully force the Enemy Empire fleet to withdraw, or perhaps even defeat them. If not, Sirah and I, Zaor and Manalia and all the others with us on this ship would never see Ares, or our home worlds again.

I came over to Quarto and spoke to him quietly. "Nice speech, will they follow your orders?"

"Yes, Jon Kirk, I believe they will, for they have no choice in an attack such as this. My leadership—any leadership—is acceptable rather than none at all. Or chaos and defeat. I just wonder where Lord Doom has gone off to, and what he is up to."

"My thoughts exactly, Quarto. Is there a way we can locate him? Sensors, perhaps? Is still aboard this vessel?" I asked, wondering where the mysterious Sindaki lord had disappeared to, and what he was planning. For I was sure he was up to no good!

"Sensors will not work on a Sindaki lord, Jon Kirk. Only another Sindaki lord can locate a Sindaki lord once he has transposed himself into the mystery plane."

"What is this mystery plane?" I asked curious now.

"It is said to be an alternate area of existence. They say they are able to open a door into another place, I know not what that place is exactly, but they can stay there as long as they will."

"Can they come back from there?" I asked Quarto.

"Yes, they have the power to move back and forth between the mystery plane. It is like going through a door from one room into another in a very large building, or so I have been told. I am not as well versed on the Sindaki methods as some others."

"So how do we do it? How to we locate this Lord Doom and capture him?" I asked determined to track down the man—even as I had not forgotten about Tob, Crooch and Vaken either. However, Doom was the immediate threat that needed to be settled first, then those other three fiends would be found for they were far overdue for justice too and had not escaped my thoughts.

Captain Quarto gave a grim Winged-men death-head grin, shrugged, moving his large folded wings, "I do not know and I do not have the time now to think about it—we have a battle to wage, Jon Kirk."

I nodded, "You are correct, of course, Captain, but is there another Sindaki lord in your fleet? Perhaps one on another of your warships?"

Quarto turned to me and smiled, showing his dark pointed teeth, "Ah, Jon Kirk, you are wise, there is such a Sindaki lord posted on *Celestial Digression*—only one of them, by the name of Lord Kneth. Shall I have him summoned?"

"Yes, please."

A moment later we found ourselves in the heat of an enormous space battle. I could see hundreds of mammoth warships using projectile weapons and some type of laser torpedo weapons, and even what they termed as old style nuclear weapons against each other. The battle raged throughout the area orbiting the planet Ares, the world that was my home now and the world I had once liberated—but had so recently lost. I feared for how the planet would fare with this battle and these powerful weapons being used all around it. I could see that the battle in space around Ares pitted our hundred Secret Empire warships against four times that number of the war fleet of the Enemy Empire.

My companions and I watched the giant space battle in awe and astonished fascination as ships burst forward upon each other in duels of exploding incandescent power and bright burning light. Force fields and shields were up on each vessel in a vain effort to block the continual powerful, and ever growing rays of force that were thrown against it to destroy the ship. Shields held, then wavered, buckling, and eventually losing resistance to the continual pounding we were taking from the enemy energy weapons. It was an incredible thing to see ships fighting each other out here in the vast darkness of space, to see the utter destruction as ships exploded in brilliant incandescence. It was grim knowledge to know that with the death of each ship, hundreds if not thousands of beings—human and otherwise—went to their deaths with each destroyed vessel. It was a sobering thought and a terrible thing to witness. Extermination on a massive scale.

"Jon Kirk!" Quarto called out to me.

I walked over to the captain, who seemed too busy to talk, but he only pointed to the merman still seated at the communications console.

Sasheen the merman quickly told me, "Jon Kirk I have made contact with Lord Kneth on *Celestial Digression*."

"Put it through!" I shouted to the merman as I went over to his station.

There was static, then a voice came over the com and an image over the view screen, "I am here," it said simply.

"Lord Kneth," I began calmly, looking at a huge old Sindaki image on the screen. He wore bright armor that I assumed was formal Sindaki warrior attire. "I am putting forward a request approved by the fleet commander. Can you help me?"

"The proper question Jon Kirk of Ares that any Sindaki lord asks is—should I help you?"

I nodded, "I will ask my question, Lord Kneth, and I will leave it to you to give me the information once you have discovered the answer as your rule decrees. Is that not fair and according to Sindaki custom?"

I looked quickly to Captain Quarto who had given me advice on these strange comrades of his and how to speak to them properly.

There was a pause from the Sindaki. I could see Lord Kneth thinking it over. Finally he said, "What is it you wish to know, Jon Kirk?"

I spoke firmly but with respect, "The whereabouts of the Sindaki Lord Doom."

Lord Kneth made a disagreeable face. I was sure he had never expected such a question, one that surely put him in conflict—Sindaki custom versus obeying an order of the fleet commander—via my request. It was a problem because I was asking him to give important personal information to an outsider about a fellow Sindaki lord. But Lord Kneth complied and said that he would use his powers to search—and finally he said, "Jon Kirk, as a Sindaki lord, I must tell you that I am truly mystified. I can not find any essence or sign of My Lord Doom anywhere on your vessel, nor on any vessel of our fleet at all. It is most unusual."

I nodded gravely, unusual was one word for it, I could think of a few others. Then I spoke up firmly, "I have heard that the Sindaki have the power to open doors to hidden realms?"

"You are well informed, Jon Kirk," Lord Kneth said coldly. He looked uncomfortable. "Yes, we have some little powers in this area. What do you wish?"

"Can you search?"

"I can try," Lord Kneth stated calmly. He closed his eyes, and stood stock still for a full minute. All the time around our ship, the huge space battle was still going on. I just hoped that our ship and Lord Kneth's own vessel would not be hit—or even destroyed—before he told me what I wanted to know. However, we were hit several times, hit hard by power weapons, buffeted and slammed, but the shields still held—but for how long was anyone's guess.

Lord Kneth suddenly opened his eyes wide and I could see he was completely surprised and at a loss for words.

"Captain Quarto asked, "What is it, My Lord Kneth?"

"This is incredible! I had not thought it possible. It can not be true!"

I said, "Lord Kneth, you have searched everywhere inside and outside of the fleet?"

"Yes, I have, Jon Kirk."

"And did you include the planet Ares below as well?" I added.

"Yes, Jon Kirk, it was a logical place to search. Lord Doom is not on the planet surface, nor anywhere to be found."

There was an ominous silence. I began to wonder if one Sindaki lord was covering for another Sindaki lord. I decided to take a big chance. I put it that way to Lord Kneth.

Instead of being insulted, the Sindaki lord merely laughed. "Jon Kirk, we Sindaki have our own agendas, our own factions, if you understand what I mean, so when I tell you I have no sympathy with Lord Doom and his ways, you will understand that while we are all Sindaki to the bone and officers of this fleet, we are not allies in all things. He is of the 'Yes' faction, I am of the minority 'No' faction. There is serious disagreement among us."

"I see," I said guardedly.

"No, you do not, but it does matter and I am not going to explain it to you now. What else do you require from me?"

I sighed, asked carefully, "Lord Kneth, have you by any chance examined the warships of the Enemy Empire?"

Lord Kneth was visibly taken aback, apparently stunned by my very words and I could see now the insult and anger in his face at what I was implying about a high Sindaki noble. He was unhappy and angry, but he held his anger in check.

Captain Quarto looked at me nervously, indicating I should say something to smooth over my words. They had been a great insult.

"Lord Kneth, I meant no disrespect..." I stammered, trying to control the damage though something in his manner told me more than his mere angry look.

"How dare you! Lowly creature! I have answered your plea and come to your help and this is how you—"

I said sternly, "Run a check, Lord Kneth. Do it now!"

"It is a waste of time and of my powers!"

"Do it!" I barked.

Lord Kneth growled but swallowed his pride and once again closed his eyes—his mind seeking Doom across the vastness of space to peer into the warships of the enemy space fleet. Suddenly the Sindaki lord bolted upright with a start, utter astonishment shown upon his face. Astonishment and fear grabbed him firmly now.

"It can not be! Not a Sindaki lord!" he shouted in rage and broken pride.

"What is it?" Captain Quarto asked carefully, fearfully concerned.

"I cannot believe what I have seen today. But I have seen it with my own mind's eye!" Lord Kneth spoke in utter shock. "Lord Doom is undetectable to us, because he is not on your vessel, nor any vessel of our fleet. Nor is he upon the planet Ares below us. Lord Doom is on the very flagship of the Enemy Empire—and *he* is directing the enemy attack against *us*!"

There was utter silence on the bridge of Quarto's ship.

Lord Kneth was stunned, broken by the discovery. Betrayed as we all were, but the personal affront of a Sindaki lord betraying his own kind was almost too much for him to accept. It was devastating to his legendry pride, an affront to his very being and dignity. It was an insult to life itself, in Sindaki eyes.

Everyone by now upon the bridge of *Dark Night* was reeling with the implications of Lord Doom's treachery. I was strangely not surprised, as one who had encountered vast treachery since I had come to Ares at the hands of men such as Tob, Vakon, and the wily Crooch—why would not a vaulted Sindaki lord sell out his own beings, his own fleet, his own empire? Nothing shocked me anymore. It was a sad realization.

Finally Captain Quarto gave voice to the words we were all thinking, "Traitor! Dirty traitor! Lord Doom is a traitor to us all!"

There was silence on the bridge as the battle still raged outside all around us. Ships exploded into fiery brightness, incandescent brilliance, so lovely and colorful in the darkness of space, until you realized that what you were witnessing was the death of a ship—and hundreds or thousands of people—or alien beings—within that ship.

There were terrible displays of energy weapons and incredible power seeking to break through the shields of our ships and destroy the fleet. The enemy weapons were seeking the weakest links, pouring incredible power into areas where our ships were battered and broken. It seemed likely that we would lose this battle, and perhaps the war. For while our larger ships were taking out many of the enemies' smaller warships, their combined power and overwhelming numbers were taking their toll on our fleet. They were cutting out the weak links, one by one, and our ships were going down in brilliant explosions of incandescent light. I looked at my beloved Sirah and held her tightly. It seemed just a matter of time now before we would all be entering the Afterworld.

Lord Kneth regained some of his composure and spoke up, "Captain Quarto, Jon Kirk, I am afraid there is one more item I must report to you. Lord Doom is not only on the enemy flagship directing the attack against us. I now believe that his provocation to use your liberation of Ares from the Winged-men of Zar was but a pretext to bring our fleet out here in the first place—out here where it could be pounced upon and destroyed by the dark fleet of this Enemy Empire. Doom is a traitor and a spy. He has been working against us and now he has led us into a trap."

I saw Zaor swallow nervously, he looked next to me in sadness at his beloved Manalia. I knew just how he felt. Gorm cursed animatedly. Tambu only shook his massive head in anger and disbelief. We had all come so far and now the doom of Lord Doom seemed to be fully upon us all.

Sirah and Manalia held each other, but refused to let their fear show in their voices or actions, They were brave women.

Captain Quarto thanked Lord Kneth and told him to keep up his fight—that our battle was not yet lost. It was a good try. However, the Sindaki lord seemed—uninterested now. The possibility of defeat—which as a Sindaki lord he had never considered before—through treacherous treason by one of his own—had put a dampener upon his very resolve. It had affected us all, but I would never let it take control of our future while we still lived!

We were outnumbered and overwhelmed by a force of four to one. The shields on our warships had almost absorbed the maximum amount of energy possible before they would begin to buckle, and then, eventually fail. Then that would be the end of us all. I knew that it could not end like this and I resolved to do all I could to save Sirah and myself, my friends and comrades in arms, and even Captain Quarto and The Secret Empire fleet. That meant we had to destroy the fleet of the Enemy Empire and Lord Doom. It was a prospect that I looked forward to with relish. The only thing now was, how to accomplish that miracle.

CHAPTER 14

THE DEFEAT OF THE FLEET

I looked at the situation and it was certainly grave. I got an idea when the captain of my imperial bodyguard, Tor-nul came over to me and spoke in a low careful voice, "Jon Kirk, all may be lost, but I want you to know that it has been an honor to serve you as my emperor."

I smiled at the lad, he was young, eager, full of fire and fight, a great warrior. He was the best man, outside of loyal Zaor, to have at your back in any fight. I was proud of him, and told him so. Then I added, "We are not dead yet, my friend. We still live, and with life, anything is possible. Never forget that!"

"A temporary situation, My Lord. But it is such a shame to die here in the coldness of space instead of the land we love upon the planet Ares so close below us. There, if any enemy ever came at us, we could destroy them utterly with the death ray weapons—the weapons Ras-noor built upon the top of the Northern Mountains. You remember those weapons, do you not, My Lord?"

I looked at Tor-nul and nodded, he was correct, then his words came home to me with the shock of a bolt of electricity and I got an idea. I wondered if it would it work? I looked at Tor-nul curiously and I smiled at the young warrior, "Tor-nul, you may have given us the key to get our butts out of the frying pan."

Tor-nul only looked back at me with a perplexed look and said, "What is a 'butt', My Lord, and why should it be placed in what you call a 'frying pan'?"

I laughed, slapping the young warrior on the back with affection, "Another of my 'quaint Earthly expressions' as Zaor is fond of calling them, my friend. I forget sometimes that I am not with Earthmen now, but living here on far distant Ares. But the important thing is that you have given me an idea, so now let us see if it can be made to work for us."

I called out to Zaor to come with me and Tor-nul to the bridge communications station, then I asked Saheen the merman, "Is there a way that you can direct these devices to communicate with my scientist Ras-noor at his labs upon Ares?"

"What are you planning, Jon Kirk?" Captain Quarto asked curiously as he came over to me. He and his staff were desperately coordinating the defense of The Secret Empire fleet and he was having considerable trouble, another of their warships had just been blasted out of the sky. It would not be long before the ships of the Enemy Empire broke through the defense perimeter Quarto had set up. We were too outnumbered to win.

Zaor said, "I see it now! You're thinking of the death ray projector platforms you had built upon the Northern Mountains."

"Yes," I responded, some excitement growing in my voice now, for I saw that there was a possibility that if we could contact our headquarters back on Ares, we might be able to bring those weapons to bear upon the enemy warships.

I told the merman, "Sasheen, contact Ras-noor's lab on Ares and find out if the death ray projectors can be reconfigured immediately to hit the Enemy Empire warships in orbit around Ares. But not our own. Give him the coordinates as soon as he is ready."

Sahseen nodded and got to work immediately. Precious moments passed as he tried to complete the connection, meanwhile the battle raged outside the hull of our ship. A furious battle was going on all around us. Attack after attack came at us, shot after shot hit our ship, protected temporarily by our shields. The shields on *Dark Night* still held, but for how long it was anyone's guess. Other warships of The Secret Empire of The Hundred Worlds were not so lucky. One ship exploded like an incandescent flare as it and it's crew died. Lord Doom had a lot to answer for this day.

"Jon Kirk," Zaor asked me, once we had moved away from Sasheen and Quarto, in a more secluded section of the bridge, "Even *if* we get a connection with Ras-noor's people down on Ares, and they can reconfigure our death ray projectors to strike the warships of the Enemy Empire—the warships of the Enemy Empire are like us, out in deep space. Our ray weapons located on Ares will not be able to reach the enemy vessels with maximum effect."

I nodded, I knew that, but I just told him, "That may be true, my friend, but keep that bit of news under your hat for now…"

Zaor allowed a short smile, nodded, knowing my words included what was another of what he considered to be my rather quaint Earthly sayings. "Under my hat?"

I continued quickly, "That is true only if the enemy ships stay in battle formation out here in space. In deep space orbit they are relatively safe. However, if they move closer to Ares…"

"Ah, now I see," Zaor said, allowing a slow grin. "But how can we do that?"

How indeed, I thought. But I had an idea on that too now.

"Captain Quarto, you need to break off your battle immediately. Send your fleet into a low planetary orbit around Ares. Bring your ships as far down into the atmosphere of the planet's surface as you can do so safely."

"But why, Jon Kirk?" Quarto asked concerned with a move which he knew could be dangerous, but more so because he was loath to break off battle with the enemy now. To do as I asked would cause his ships to break formation, and it could make them more vulnerable to enemy power weapons until they were able to reform and set up a new defensive perimeter using overlapping shielding.

"You must do this, Captain, to save your fleet," I told him.

Quarto looked at me and explained, "My comrades and I have waited for a long time for this battle, and while it is going badly for us, I am loath to call retreat. To run is unthinkable! Defeat is bad enough, Jon Kirk, I can accept that as a warrior, as a Winged-man of Zar, but not cowardice."

"It is not cowardice, Quarto," I told him confidently, then I quickly explained to him my plan.

He listened, nodded, then gave me a toothy Zaran smile, "It may just work."

"Jon Kirk! Jon Kirk!" It was Sasheen the merman shouting from his communications station full of excitement. "I have done it! I have made voice contact with Ras-noor's assistant, Von-bar, and he assures me that he can reconfigure all the platform weapons as you desire. He awaits your orders to fire."

"And what of the telescopic sites?" I asked Sasheen quickly, "Ask Von-bar if they can distinguish between Secret Empire and Enemy Empire warships in low Ares orbit."

Sahseen relayed that message, and an instant later he responded, "Yes, Von-bar says he can do that, but you must get the targets closer to Ares for the power of his weapons to achieve maximum effect."

I nodded, I knew what that meant, "Tell him to stand by."

Then I looked over at Captain Quarto, "So you see. It can be done. Now it is up to you. Move fast, my friend!"

Captain Quarto swallowed harshly, "Yes, My Lord, Jon Kirk, I will do it your way. Gorm, Tambu, order our fleet to break off their attack immediately. Tell all ships to break formation, and head for a new battle formation in low orbit around the planet Ares. I will transfer the pattern now. Sasheen, contact all the fleet captains and order them to follow our lead without hesitation!"

Instantly dozens of massive warships of The Secret Empire of The Hundred Worlds, under the command of Captain Quarto-Zar, and Jon Kirk of Ares, broke off their battle with the hundreds of remaining warships of the Enemy Empire under the Emperor of the Known Universe. The retreat was orderly and quick but it proved costly for two of our warships that were blown out of the atmosphere once they left formation. However, Quarto held a tight reign on his fleet, and soon it was back in formation and in low orbit around the planet Ares.

Moments later hundreds of war vessels of the Enemy Empire, that had chased our ships thinking we were retreating and smelling the blood of our easy defeat, were also entering low orbit around Ares where they continued their attack upon our fleet. The damage upon our side was increasing now, and the ships of the enemy came in closer for the kill. That was just where I wanted them to be. If we could but hold out a little longer—until they were all here!

"Sasheen! What is Von-bar doing? Tell him to step it up! Now!" I shouted.

The merman passed my order, looked sad, then despondent. "I can not get through, Jon Kirk, the enemy is jamming our cvommunications."

I nodded, it was expected this low in the atmosphere. I just hoped and prayed that Von-bar was ready and would act soon. Very soon! As we were in dire straights.

"Von-bar has the coordinates?" I asked the merman.

"Yes, Jon Kirk," Sasheen replied.

Now I knew the real battle would begin.

Suddenly massive rays of burning incandescent fire leaped out from a hundred points on the planetary surface of Ares. Power rays shot into the darkness of the upper atmosphere blasting the attacking warships of the Enemy Empire. The enemy ships were surrounded by incandescent beams of force, ensconced by them, overwhelmed by the power beams. No warship could withstand such force. There were soon many massive explosions as a hundred planetary rays hit the same amount of enemy ships and caused them to transform into blazing brilliant death fires. The destruction was immediate and devastating.

Now was the time for our fleet join in, and the combination of the weapons from the planet's surface with our own fleet firepower, was first damaging, and then destroying the attacking enemy ships quickly one by one. Their shields were quickly overwhelmed by the massive surge of force, first they buckled, and then they broke. There were explosions that lit up the planet like a flare, and I remembered it all as if it were some kind of massive fireworks display.

Sirah and I stood together in each other's arms on the bridge of *Dark Night* and watched the slow but constant destruction of the warships of the attackers known as the Enemy Empire. Ship after ship went down to destruction. I only hoped it would prove to be Lord Doom's doom as well. I prayed that one of those ships crashing down to Ares to destruction or exploding into nothingness, had Lord Doom upon it.

The planetary ray platform projectors from Ares turned the trick. Their massive power and size created a devastating force that crashed into the shields of the Enemy Empire warships, overwhelming their defenses, then exploding their vessels, breaking their fighting formation, making them easy prey for our ships to pick off. The enemy was losing ship after ship now. It was glorious.

"There goes another one!" Zaor shouted in glee.

"Two more over here!" Gorm growled with happy rage. "Blown clear out of the sky!"

However, the enemy was not that easily beaten, for as each Enemy Empire warship was destroyed, another vessel took it's place in the battle formation, and yet even it soon was also destroyed. The more of their ships that were destroyed, the faster the pace of that destruction proceeded, until the Enemy Empire fleet was entirely decimated. Our vessels were now safe and able to enjoy a brief respite from the carnage. It must soon become apparent to even the most die-heard partisan of the Enemy Empire fleet that they had been lured into a trap and that their battle was lost.

"They are trapped now," Quarto observed with a flapping of his large wings with excitement. "If they do not withdraw immediately, they may not have any warships left to withdraw."

I nodded, watching the destruction, hugging Sirah tightly to me, "Soon, my beloved, we will be back home again and safe on Ares."

"I have always been safe, Jon Kirk, as long as I am in your arms," she told me with a soft smile. "But it will be nice to be back home again and to see our son."

I looked at her lovingly, "That's my baby!"

"Look!" Zaor shouted, he was standing at an observation window with Manalia at his side. "They are moving off!"

"They have no choice now," Captain Quarto offered with a pure grimace of Zaran Winged-man joy and battle triumph.

Sirah and I watched in awe and relief as the few remaining warships of the Enemy Empire fleet disengaged themselves from the battle and began to limp away through the upper atmosphere of Ares to escape into outer space.

Quarto barked out, "Sasheen, order all captains and vessels of our fleet to run down the Enemy Empire ships and destroy them! Do not let them get away!"

There was a sudden massive explosion on one of the enemy warships.

Zaor shouted, "Look! That was the Enemy Empire flagship blown to bits!"

A cheer rang up on the bridge of *Dark Night*, but it was quelled by instantaneous darkness and corresponding fear. The lights suddenly went out, all controls and power were dead. And something else. There was the feeling of something evil having come aboard our ship. It was uncanny and inexplicable, but most on the bridge felt the feeling surrounding them and some commented upon it. It was almost suffocating. The darkness and loss of energy had us all frantically trying to reestablish power and control. Suddenly the lights went on again and our ship's power had been restored. I looked at Captain Quarto, he shook his head and flapped his wings in the negative, indicating that it had not been he nor his staff who had restored the lights and power.

Then I saw before me a fearsome apparition, the face and form of Lord Karlath Doom himself.

"Jon Kirk," his Sindaki voice boomed with eerie dread menace, "you have interfered with my plans for the last time. Your success on Ares was useful to my plans initially, so I did not interfere with it. It was you becoming emperor of that puny country of green-skinned creatures, freeing it from the Winged-men of Zar, that offered just the excuse I needed to raise this Secret Empire of The Hundred Worlds war fleet. Once that was accomplished—I could betray it for unimaginable power to my new benefactor—He Whose Name is Never To Be Spoken, but is called The Emperor of The Known Universe! Now our plans are set in motion. This battle is just a minor setback. You can not comprehend our forces. The main battle lies ahead. Utter destruction will result. No surrender will be accepted. Your time will come soon, Jon Kirk!"

I had heard and seen enough and knew what must be done. I immediately drew my sword and rammed it to the hilt into the form of Lord Doom, directly *into* the vile creature's heart—and to my surprise—directly *through* it as well. There was a harsh laugh and the image of Lord Doom suddenly disappeared from the bridge of *Dark Night*.

There was silence, terror and stark relief upon the bridge.

Where Lord Doom had disappeared to no one knew. I realized that his presence was just some kind of projection, similar to what I had used to contact my friend on Earth years ago using Tar-gool's space machine. I wondered, did Lord Doom have some type of machine as well? Were the great Sindaki powers and magic just projections of some type of super machine? Not magic, but super science? I did not know yet what to think. I had too many questions and not enough answers.

"We need answers," I said firmly. I had Sasheen contact our Sindaki ally Lord Kneth, but he could still not determine Lord Doom's location.

"He is not on any of our ships, nor on the planet surface of Ares, so he may still be upon one of the fleeing Enemy Empire ships," Lord Kneth told us.

I nodded, held Sirah tightly looking into her eyes, "He is gone and we have won the battle this day. His image here was just that, only an image, a projection, nothing more. Nothing substantial. Soon we will be back home in Tarcos."

"I love you, Jon Kirk," Sirah told me as she kissed me lightly upon the lips. I kissed her back and a wild cheer of applause and victory went up from all hands onboard the bridge of that mighty space-faring warship.

"Jon Kirk," Captain Quarto came over to us and bowed most gallantly to me, it was almost embarrassing. "It has been an honor to serve with you in such a victory."

"The honor has been mine, Captain," I replied truthfully. Seeing his huge winged body and his ugly monster features twisted in respect, and perhaps even friendship, was something new for me to see in any Zaran. Even so, it gave me hope for the future.

Quarto then continued, "I will let you and your people off upon planet Ares, then I shall take any others who wish to go, back to their own home worlds. Their *consignat* service to The Secret Empire is ended. Those who will follow me willingly will form a new fleet, with the support of Lord Kneth and the Sindaki, and we will hunt down Lord Doom and defeat him and the Enemy Empire of this self-styled Emperor of The Known Universe. I am sure it will prove to be such a battle as we have never seen before. I am a changed warrior of Zar this day. I have seen such things now I had never contemplated before. I will not serve our enemies ever again. You have given me much food for thought, on many subjects, Jon Kirk. Perhaps we shall meet each other again? Perhaps we shall be allies once again?"

"I will look forward to that day, Captain," I said, then a cheer went up on the bridge from a hundred voices, out of the mouths of beings from a dozen different worlds.

CHAPTER 15

EMPEROR JON KIRK

That night Sirah and I lay safely sleeping once again in our comfortable bed in our apartment in the palace of the capital city of Tarcos upon the planet Ares. We had come home and we were happy after being through so much war and travail.

Earlier that day I had ordered Captain Quarto to use his warships to remove all Winged-men occupiers and their Blue Korta allies from the six cities of Ares and all the lands under the Green Empire. The Zaran captain had done as I asked and these occupiers were now gone from our world and all of our six cities were free once again. The green people moved back to their cities and rejoiced. It had been a busy day.

I awoke as Sirah stirred furtively. I could tell she was still upset by the events we had been thorugh.

"What is it, beloved?" I asked, drawing my sword, which I always kept at the ready these days in a spot on the floor beside our bed. Danger always seemed to swirl around us and a trusty blade was a good thing to have handy. The chamber was dark, and seemed uninhabited save for Sirah and myself. These days on Ares I knew that did not mean anything either. I was contemplating calling some of Tor-nul's Black Dragons, my palace guard, when Sirah turned to me and in wide-eyed terror pointed past me to an image standing in front of the far wall behind us.

I looked where she pointed and saw that it was the image of a man. Instantly, sword in hand, I placed Sirah squarely behind me for her protection, for I could see that the man was the Sindaki madman magician, Lord Karlath Doom—or more accurately—some kind of projection or holographic image of him. It was a very effective trick, very realistic, it appeared that he was right there in the room with us.

He stood boldly across the room from us without any seeming regard for his life or safety. He had the look of bloody murder in his eyes. The hatred in him was beyond all recognition, it was something we could feel, it was evil, it was relentless.

I quickly moved Sirah behind me and called for the guards at once just to be on the safe side. One could never know what mischief such a fiend had in mind.

Then Lord Doom's voice spoke in a eerie deadly tone:

I have not forgotten you, Jon Kirk! I think of you constantly. I shall be back when I am done consolidating my power here, and once I am ready, you, your family and your world shall feel my wrath—and the wrath of my great master—the being whose name can not be mentioned but who is known as the Emperor of The Known Universe! Be forewarned, your terrible end is coming and I shall savor it!

I shouted again for my guards, who now came instantly, but by then the image had melted away as if made of mist and it was gone.

Sirah stifled a scream. "Was he here? In our very bedroom?"

"No, it was not him, it was only an image. It was not real," I assured her.

"But he seemed so real!" she cried in near panic. I could not blame her for being upset, I was pretty shook up too by this visitation into our most private living area.

"I know, but it was not real. Just an image, that is all. Do not worry about it, my love," I said, holding her closer to me. "We are safe. Trust me, I will not let him harm us or our son."

I saw Sirah reluctantly nod and then put her own dagger away back into the folds of her sleeping silks, but I could see that the entire episode had really upset her. It had done the same for me as well. Then she immediately ran into the adjoining room to check on our son, Alun. He was fine and unharmed.

With Sirah with our son, I was left with a creepy feeling that came over me—not because of Lord Doom's fearful image, fearful as it was—but because of what he had admitted to me so openly in his little speech. He had told me that he would be back for me, but only after he had consolidated his power. I tossed and turned that around in my mind all that night wondering what he could mean by that. Doom had betrayed his own people, the magical Sindaki lords, and they were now after him. I knew Lord Kneth, with now Admiral of the Fleet Quarto-Zar, were looking for the traitor together to bring him to justice for his treachery against the Sindaki.

Then a chill ran through my body and it came to me—the reason why Doom had mentioned to me that he must consolidate his power *first* before he came after me. That was because the only beings who were any real threat to him were those same Sindaki lords whom he had betrayed. That meant he had to destroy them before they could destroy him. And I was afraid now that meant Lord Doom was going to destroy his own home planet of Sindaki and murder everyone on that world! It was a fantastic thought, but I would put nothing past such a monster. I feared that just might be his twisted plan.

I was frantic about this realization, and as I worked it over and over in my head, I came out with the same dire result. It made sense. It could be true. He would naturally go after the biggest threat to him first. That is what Doom must be planning now, and once he had the Sindaki threat neutralized, then he would come for me and the people of Ares.

I did not sleep much that night for images of Lord Doom haunted my dreams. I feared for Sirah and my little son, Alun. I feared for Ares and my people. For I knew Doom's revenge once taken against me, would not be against me alone. It would be against my entire family, my city, and the entire world and the people of Ares. Something had to be done to stop him before it was too late. The next morning I summoned all my advisors and ministers for a great war council. There had to be some way to trap this Sindaki lord and end his treachery?

The Grand Audience Chamber in the palace at Tarcos was huge and held many of the leaders of the Green Empire. I had sent word for them all to be at this meeting. There was First Minister Sahn Jor; General Zaor; wise Ar-den; old scientist Ras-noor; and dozens of others. Tor-nul of my Black Dragons bodyguard was also present.

I explained to all there what had happened the night before. I told them of the threat this Lord Karlath Doom posed to Ares, myself, Sirah and our son—but also the Sindaki lords of the other worlds that made up The Secret Empire. While I had no loyalty to this Secret Empire, I did feel positively to Lord Kneth and Admiral Quarto-Zar. I also realized that if the two empires fought and The Secret Empire lost, then Lord Doom and his master—this alien entity called the Emperor of the Known Universe would be in control of everyone and everything in known space. That was bad for me and bad for Ares. I much better liked the strategy of playing one empire against the other, which allowed an apparently unimportant planet like little Ares more say-so in its own future. Or better yet, to just be left alone as the big guys fought amongst themselves.

So what do we do?" Zaor asked carefully.

"I will hold a meeting here in two days time for all the leaders from all over Ares." I said. "Shan Jor, make sure that King Konor of the Blues is here also."

Sahn Jor nodded, then added, "Should I invite Shamar and Aron of Keva—or those of the new city called Kev?"

"Can you even find this hidden city?"

"No, I have no idea where it may be, and they will not allow anyone near it" Shan Jor replied resignedly.

"And even if you are able to find their city somehow, you could never convince them to help us, you know that," I stated matter-of-factly.

"Yes, that is true, My Emperor."

"So we should forget about the Kevans, it would be great to have them on our side helping us, but we do not have the time to find them and convince them to join us. Events are moving too fast. We need to come up with a plan that will stop Lord Doom. Something. Anything! There must be some way we can trap him when he comes here to get his revenge against me, or to track him down and find out where he is now. Then we can go after him and bring him down. We also need to find a way to warn the Sindalki lords of the danger they are in. They are his next target. I believe their world, their home planet is in great danger."

Ras-noor stood up, the wily old scientist said, "My Lord, we still have a small scout flier, we could send a messenger in it to The Secret Empire fleet, they may not be too far away yet for the small scout ship to reach them."

"Then do that immediately," I ordered.

Shan Jor stood up, "Jon Kirk, I advise that you and your family move out of the capital. Perhaps to the safety of the Caves of Conscience. You are a target here in Tarcos and are in great danger."

I nodded, "I know I am a target, we are all targets, Sahn Jor. Lord Doom was very clear in his threat the other night. He is coming for me, my family and my world. That means he will take revenge on Ares itself. We are all in danger. Please, all of you think about what was spoken here and try to come up with something I can use to stop this madman."

* * * *

Two days later the Grand Audience Chamber of the palace in Tarcos was abuzz with leaders from the four corners of the planet Ares.

All my ministers, generals and scientists where at the meeting. The governors of all six cities of the Green Empire were there. Konor, King of the Blues from the western continent was in attendance. It was good to see him again.

Once again I gave the details of the problem and asked for suggestions on what we could do to defeat Lord Doom before he made his move against us. I knew that the best bet to stop Doom was the warships of The Secret Empire fleet, and that meant we needed to hear from Captain—now, Admiral Quarto-Zar. So far there had been no reply to the scout ship I had sent out to contact him two days ago. Our ship never came back and I do not believe our messenger was ever able to contact the fleet. Perhaps he never found the fleet—or the Enemy Empire ships found him? Things looked grim. As it turned out, they would only get grimmer.

Zaor had the floor. He was speaking about the possibility of taking captured Vognar planetary warships and converting them into interplanetary warships, when the sounds of screams and wild panic first came to our ears. It appeared they were resounding throughout the entire city. The attention of everyone at the meeting now was cut sharply as we all looked to each other wondering what this could mean. It sounded like chaos had suddenly overcome the city and I feared we might be under attack. I alerted the guards.

Then Tor-nul crashed into the audience chamber with a dozen armed Black Dragons bodyguard and I knew something serious was up. "My Lord, look to the sky. There is a ship here. A very big one!"

I didn't know what that might mean but I would find out. I walked out onto the terrace and was astounded to see that above the city of Tarcos was a large black ship hanging stationary above the city like an ominous dark shadow. It looked like it might be a Secret Empire warship, but it could just as easily be an enemy vessel, they all looked the same and it was so hard to tell them apart from so far away.

"At least they have not fired upon us yet, so maybe it is not Lord Doom, or any enemy ship," Zaor offered.

"Yes, that may be," I replied cautiously. I considered ordering an immediate evacuation of the city, but that was perhaps too premature. In any event, it would not save the people of Tarcos from bombardment. I called out the guard—for what it was worth—for there was no way we could fight an interplanetary warship if it decided to attack Tarcos. Maybe we here in Tarcos could not fight such a ship, but we had another way. I quickly called over Ras-noor, "Contact your people and have them ready the platform projectors. If that ship is an enemy vessel and shows the least hostility, you are to blow it out of the sky."

"Yes, My Lord!" and Ras-noor was off to prepare the weapons.

"Look, Jon Kirk," my advisor Ar-den added, "the ship is sending out a smaller ship from it, and that smaller ship is heading down toward the plains in front of Tarcos to land."

He was right. Whoever it was, it appeared they wanted to talk. At least they were not shooting, and if they wanted to talk that was good by me, talk was good and I could wait. We watched as the ship flew through the atmosphere of Ares and then finally came to land on the flat plains before Tarcos. Once the ship opened up it suddenly spewed forth two long columns of fierce heavily armed Blue Korta shock troops. The Kortas then spread out to create a space between the two long columns.

What was this now?

"It seems like some kind of honor guard," Zaor surmised.

"Or perhaps the pinpoint of Lord Dooms invasion force?" Sahn Jor countered.

I looked closely at the image through my telescope. They were Blue Kortas all right, and there were a lot of them. What were they doing here? They had just left Ares a couple of days ago—now they were back!

Then I saw a huge Winged-man exit the ship. Was it Quarto? Could it be him? Most Zarans looked alike to me, and even with a telescope I could not tell for sure, so far away was he from me. Then I saw others who followed behind the large Zaran, and my heart jumped for joy when I could easily see the huge Viking-like Gorm, with his perpetual companion Tambu at his side. I thought they had been taken back to their home world? What were they doing here now? I had a lot of questions bubbling up inside me the more I watched the procession coming out from that ship.

I sighed with relief, "They are friends and allies. It is Admiral Quarto."

A cheer went up from the assembly with that realization, and we all watched as the procession grew and began its approach to the wall of the city. I noticed others also in the group that were coming towards the city. There was Bran, Sharn, Sasheen, Poln and many others. I was surprised to see them all here once again. I thought all would surely be back on their home worlds by now. I wonder what had brought them all together again—and here to Ares!

"Zaor, take a detachment of Black Dragons and escort our guests here immediately," I ordered.

"Yes, My Lord," Zaor replied and soon he and Tor-nul were off to bring our visitors into the palace and to the council meeting.

Sahn Jor came over to me offering up a grim smile, "And now we shall see what we shall see."

I smiled, "You are being enigmatic again, my friend."

"These do seem the times for such ways of thinking."

"Indeed, so what do you make of this unannounced visit?"

"Nothing good, I fear," Sahn Jor replied. "Our scout ship with the messenger I sent—well I am sure he did not get through to the fleet. This can not be any reply to that message. This must be something else."

I nodded, "I figure the same. Trouble is brewing and it goes by the name of Lord Karlath Doom. I am afraid he is on the way here."

"But the Sindalki lords? Surely he must deal with them first, as you explained? It makes sense that they would want to deal with his treachery immediately. They should be after him, he may not have any place to hide now."

"Yes, but unless I miss my guess, Lord Doom has already dealt with them in some way. Perhaps he has forged some kind of alliance? I would not put it past him, or those corrupt power-hungry lords to make some deal with him and look the other way on his treachery. It is called power politics, Sahn Jor, and it seems to be just as prevalent here as on my home world of Earth."

Sahn Jor nodded sadly, "Well we shall not have long to wait. Zaor and Tor-nul will be back here soon enough with our visitors."

"Yes, we shall hear about it all soon enough, for good or ill."

It was minutes later when the doors to the palace audience chamber suddenly burst open and Zaor and Tor-nul, accompanied by a group of my Black Dragons, escorted our visitors into the room in a rather majestic and long procession made up of many friends and allies. It was good to see them all again, but as they came forward I could see the worry etched upon the faces of each and every one of them. I knew this was no social visit. I also knew that many of them had wanted to be taken back to their home worlds after the recent battle—the fact that they were not back on their home worlds and were here now, seemed very ominous. I was rather surprised to even see among them the noble Sindalki, Lord Kneth—though he did not look quite right to me—something seemed very wrong with him. An illness of some kind? That also concerned me.

Admiral Quarto-Zar led the group as they came over to me and my ministers and officials. Everyone was introduced. I noted a large Blue Korta named General Zod was brought forward, bowed, he was introduced by Quarto as the military leader of all the Kortas serving in the empire. I was surprised to see a Korta serving in Quarto's force and told him so.

"Emperor Jon Kirk," Quarto spoke in his powerful Winged-man voice so all could hear, "It is good to see you again, My Lord. We have all joined together in this important mission to meet with you."

"Well, it is good to see again too, my friend," I replied meaning it, smiling, but wondering what he was doing here. What was so important that he and all these leaders were here now? Why was he not out with his fleet looking for Lord Doom? "What can I do for you?"

"When last we left each other a mere few days ago, I expressed the desire that I hoped we would some day see each other again, and that perhaps I would fight by your side once more. I believe we are at that moment in time now."

I nodded, that was certainly dire enough, "Tell me, what has happened?"

"Everything," Quarto said with a dark grimace. Then he began to tell his story. "After we left Ares, my fleet met the Enemy Empire fleet and fought it to a standstill. It was a massive and long battle, many casualties. We lost some ships and crews, but we persisted. I thought we had given a good account of ourselves, at least we had thwarted their advance into this part of Known Space, and they had to withdraw. It seemed a victory, of sorts at the time. However, what we did not know was while we were fighting part of their fleet, the rest of it under Lord Doom was already in orbit around the Sindalki home world. They destroyed the Sindalki planet, killing all the Sindalki—only Lord Doom survives his victory—and Lord Kneth who was with my fleet and is now only a mere shell of the man he once was—the destruction of his people has caused his fine mind extreme harm and his mighty powers wain."

I looked at Lord Kneth. He stood like a statue, frozen and cold, unseeing and unfeeling. He was in mourning for his planet, his people, his race. Lord Kneth looked like one of the living dead, a man who had given up on life and who was merely awaiting death and cold dark eternity to take him.

"I am sorry," I said, astounded by the extent of the crime—an entire race of beings destroyed—an entire planet destroyed! And Doom had done it to his own world! What kind of a monster was he?

"Sorrow, yes," Quarto agreed. "However, the loss of the Sindalki lords to us means much more than a horrible crime against the Lord of Life, for now there is nothing and no one to stop Lord Doom and his master from achieving their evil aims. They will conquer us all. If that happens it will be the death of us all, a hundred races, a thousand planets will become absorbed into a vast slave empire that make the harsh Sindalki lords look compassionate by comparison."

"I understand, but perhaps you are exaggerating the danger? In any event I have my own reasons for wanting to defeat Doom, but what can I do to help you? You have the entire fleet at your disposal to hunt him down. I have no space ships, no space army."

"Not so much of a fleet any more, I am afraid, My Emperor."

I looked at him sharply and could read the sadness and fear he held within.

"Tell me everything, my friend," I asked, looking at him and then each face of my visitors that filled the huge chamber.

Admiral Quarto stepped forward, nodded, then began to address all in the huge chamber, "To begin, I must tell you all here the history of the two empires. The one I serve—which may no longer exist with the death of the Sindalki lords—and the other. Two space-faring empires, each initially unknown to the other, met and made war upon each other about a hundred years ago. We call ourselves the First Empire, because we think of ourselves as being first—we call the other the Enemy Empire, simply because they are an empire that is our enemy. It is just names, just words. The official name of our space empire is The Secret Empire of The Hundred Worlds—it was run by the Sindalki lords who did not seek ultimate control over the worlds they ruled. They ruled through surrogates, through local leaders who paid tribute to the Sindalki in wealth, raw materials and military levies for the fleet to defend the empire. They did not overly interfere in the life of locals who they ruled. They cared little about them so long as tribute flowed to them. In fact, most locals had no idea their world was ruled by our masters at all, hence the name Secret Empire, and that is just the way the Sindalki lords wanted it."

I looked at Quarto knowingly, the history lesson all sounded familiar. I had seen this kind of thing before, in Earth history, with Ancient Rome. Rome had been a template for a successful empire—but now The Secret Empire was gone with the death of the Sindalki rulers. So now what was coming in its place?

"Now what of this other empire?" I asked firmly.

"That is a problem for great concern," Quarto explained, looking at all the faces in the huge palace chamber. "It is what we call the Second Empire—or the Enemy Empire—but it is not as simple as all that. It is something quite different from what we have been able to determine. The Sindalki lords were working on the problem of who or what these enemies are and how to fight them, and they were making some progress before their demise. They were exterminated because they posed a threat to this Enemy Empire. What exactly it is, we do not know. It is very different from our reality, from what we know and think of. But we do know a few things, the overlord master is called He Who is Not To Be Named, ominous, is it not?"

"Yes, but it is just a name, Quarto—or not even a name. Just a collection of words. Words do not scare me," I said boldly. I saw some of the men in that chamber nod their heads in agreement with me.

"That is true, My Emperor" the winged Admiral continued with a sly leer. I could see that he was working up to the real reason for his visit here today. "The master of the enemy is called Kin-Ty-Roo. We do not know what that means. We do not know if he is even a 'he', or even a being like us at all. I think not. Our scientists presume it is some type of alien entity. The problem is, that without the Sindalki lords, we now have no leaders, no focal point to rally our forces and no power to oppose this enemy who calls itself Emperor of the Known Universe."

I nodded, "I see that. Well, I can think of no one better qualified to lead the fleet and the worlds of The Secret Empire, than you, Admiral Quarto."

Quarto reeled backwards in actual horror and shock at my words, "Oh, no, My Lord! Not I. Never I!"

I looked hard at the winged creature and my new friend. If you would have told me bare weeks ago that I would respect and even become friends with a Zaran Winged-man you would have been able to knock me over with a feather. But I now considered Quarto a friend and a most effective leader. However, he seemed adamant on not taking the leadership role. I wondered why? If not he, then who? Lord

Kneth seemed a logical one to turn to, but he hardly seemed able, he appeared to be seriously ill.

I shrugged, "Well, I am afraid I do not understand, you are already admiral of the fleet. You are the leader of the empire, de facto now, or at least the part that matters, you control the military forces."

Quarto shook his head sadly, "I am afraid The Secret Empire no longer exists, Jon Kirk. With the death of the Sindalki, the empire is dead. It is time for something more. Something different. Something new is needed to replace it."

"I agree, and you are the one to lead that new—empire—or whatever you want to call it," I stated simply.

"No, My Emperor, what I do is more than enough for me. I will continue to serve until we defeat Doom and this Enemy Empire, but then I shall go home to Zar and raise winglets and forget all about war and violence. It disgusts me."

I looked from Quarto all around the room at all the other leaders in attendance. I saw Konor from Vognar and his Blues of Ares; the space pirate Bran from Ko-Ah-Leh; the large Viking-like Gorm of the Gorms and his companion, Tambu; Sharn of the tall yellow Tergats; Sasheen the merman from Talu; Poln the *felina* tiger creature; I spotted General Zod—well there was no way I would allow a Blue Korta general to become leader. I wished that Shamar and Aron of Keva were here to offer their suggestions and wise council.

I looked over at Admiral Quarto again, "Well, I can tell that you have some plan, so tell me, what have you decided?"

Admiral Quarto smiled and bowed in sincere respect, "My Emperor, Jon Kirk, we will soon be in a life and death struggle with the being who calls itself the Emperor of the Known Universe. We need our own emperor to oppose it, to rally behind, to fight for—but most of all we need a great leader to lead us. Jon Kirk, you are Emperor of the Green Empire of Ares, you are Emperor of Ares—now it is time for you to pick up the mantle given to you by those who need you most—become our emperor, become the Emperor of The Known Universe!"

I looked directly at Quarto and tried to hold back a laugh. Was he serious? I think he was serious! I was stunned. I laughed again lightly now, quite amused. I barely knew what to say, but then replied, "That is a good joke, my friend, but you can not really be serious? Let me tell you with all sincerity that I neither seek nor will accept any such honor."

"Is there nothing we could offer you to make you take the Emperorship?"

"Hah! Please do not continue with this. You could not pay me enough."

"Nothing would make you take the title of Emperor of the Known Universe, nothing including saving the life of your wife and young son, and of saving Ares itself. Think about that. And Jon Kirk, while you now consider yourself a man of Ares—you are after all, an Earthman…"

"So what does Earth have to do with anything?" I asked sharply.

"Better you should ask me how Lord Doom knows of Earth. You said he promised that he would return to destroy you, your family, *and your world?*"

"Yes," I replied carefully, "those were his exact words."

"Well, what is your world, Jon Kirk?" Quarto asked firmly.

"Ares, of course," I replied simply.

Quarto snorted derisively, "No. I am sorry, My Lord. You are not *of* Ares. You are an Earthman, you were always an Earthman, and you will always be an Earthman regardless of where you live or rule."

"What are you trying to tell me, Quarto?"

"Your lovely little blue world of Earth will surely go the same way as the Sindalki world has gone if Doom is not defeated and this Kin-Ty-Roo, this so-called Emperor of the Known Universe is not usurped by a better man. That better man is you, Jon Kirk."

"I am not better, I am not a good…"

"It does not matter." Quarto told me sternly. "You are the best we have. You are the one who can unite us, you are the only one who can lead us and who all here will follow. You are the one those here will die for if need be! Jon Kirk, you are the only one all here can agree upon as our Emperor. We have already decided!"

I just shook my head sadly, I could not believe it. No one had consulted me on this! It was bad enough being appointed ruler of the Greens, and now of Ares—but what was it they had called me? Emperor of the Known Universe? That was ridiculous! It was a ridiculous title. I said as much.

Quarto would not hear of it, instead he chanted, "All hail, Jon Kirk, Emperor of The Green Empire, Emperor of Ares, and now Emperor of The Known Universe!"

The cheers that rang up actually hurt my ears they were so loud and frantic. Everyone seemed delighted by the idea. I wondered why.

I certainly was not. I could not figure it out. There was not a silent voice in that vast chamber, many thousands cheered enthusiastically. Not one voice opposed. It was stunning, incredible. I was so embarrassed. Of course I could not accept, but I did not what to insult them for the honor they wanted to bestow upon me—however ill conceived.

I stood up tall and straight, looking into every face and seeing their hope and bright eyes anticipating what I was going to tell them, and knowing I was going to disappoint them all. It was a sad undertaking. I took a deep breath and surged ahead trying to be respectful and serious, "I thank you all, my friends, for the great honor you have offered me here today."

There were more wild cheers and applause. I shook my head and held my hands up for them to quiet down. It took a while. Finally I was able to continue.

"I do appreciate this great honor, it is an amazing tribute, but I must decline your offer. I am not the man for such a lofty position. I am merely a man, and only a fighting man at that, not some prince or politician. I am afraid I would serve you poorly. So I must tell you that I can not accept such an honor."

There were sounds of great disappointment.

"No, you are the one, Jon Kirk! You must accept!" I now heard a new voice speak clearly to me, but it was not a physical voice that any others there heard—it was a voice inside my head only I heard. It sounded like Aron of Keva. *"Look over here and you shall see us."*

I startled, looked to the left as indicated, saw all the faces, and was startled to see two men slowly walking toward me from the back of the room. It was young King Shamar of Keva, and with him was Aron The Eldest of the Old Ones of Keva—or as it was now called, Kev.

"Aron! Shamar, my friends!" I shouted in joy. "You are here? It is so good to see you both!"

"We are here, and it good to see you again, Jon Kirk," Aron stated simply. Then he looked at me seriously, "We are here because you must take up the mantle, you must accept the title of Emperor of the Known Universe. In doing so you shall save us all. You will save your wife and child, save Ares, save your Earth, and save all those here from what is coming and seeks to devour us all."

I looked carefully at Aron, then to Shamar. I did not know what to say to them.

"You must accept, Jon Kirk," Shamar stated seriously. "You are being called, we all need you."

"But…but I can not, I am not worthy," I replied, growing frantic that all this was being thrust upon me. It was so sudden, so unexpected. It was one thing being Emperor of Ares, but this was just too amazing. I did not see it as a power gain for me as some might have, I saw it as a great and drastic responsibility, a heavy burden I feared I would not be able to shoulder.

Aron smiled broadly, "I know you do not see the Emperorship as a power gain but as a great and drastic responsibility, a heavy burden you believe you would not be able to shoulder."

"Are you repeating my thoughts back to me, Aron?"

"Yes, and that is why you are worthy, because I can see that you do not seek the power. You detest it. You see it as a burden. That is a good quality to have in any leader, Jon Kirk. It is why you must take the Emperorship and lead us against this new enemy. You are the only one who can do it. We have all decided, all have agreed. You are the one. If you refuse, we all die a terrible death," Aron told me sincerely. "Sometimes, my friend, we must take on the responsibilities we do not want in order to save everything that we love and hold dear."

I sighed sadly, I was thinking it through. I did not want to be responsible for the death of my family, for the destruction of Ares, or Earth, and so many other worlds by not doing what I in my heart now knew that I needed to do. Even Zar would be gone. So many worlds, I could only guess at their inhabitants, all would be gone. The planets of the Tergats, the worlds of Bran, Gorm, Sasheen, Poln, even the Kortas. Someone had to stop this from happening. It now appeared that someone was me. I could lead them.

I would lead them!

Aron looked me in the eyes, "Yes, Jon Kirk, they will all be gone, absorbed into the Kin-Ty-Roo, if you do not lead us to victory."

"Is that why you have come here? To force this duty upon me?"

The wise man allowed a slight smile, "I and the Old Ones of Kev have been monitoring you. When I saw you would not take the Emperorship being offered by Admiral Quarto, I knew I must come here myself and make you accept it. Shamar came with me. You have no choice, my friend, I am sorry. You are needed. It is necessary. It shall be done."

"But Emperor of the Known Universe? Really? That is quite a mouthful, a silly extravagant title."

Aron smiled, then nodded his head, "Yes, but it is just a title, just words, nothing more. What is important is what you *do*—not the name you are *called*. What title you will have is not important. What you will *do* is lead us all in our fight for freedom from extinction—for I have seen what this Kin-Ty-Roo really is—an alien entity with an all-devouring hunger that must be defeated!"

I had never heard Aron speak so firmly and with such conviction upon any subject before. For him to physically leave Kev and come here to Tarcos to speak with me—for him to force me to take on the Emperorship—I knew he had seen something that had shaken him to his very core. I knew then that a terrible war was coming and I now found myself right in the middle of it. He said I had no choice. So be it!

"My beloved husband." I looked up and saw the lovely Lady Sirah, my Empress and the love of my life approaching.

I had not seen Sirah enter the chamber. She now stood before me dressed in a shimmering white gown, upon her waist was belted a long sword in a jeweled scabbard. She looked at me with a little mischievous smile.

"You have heard?" I asked.

She smiled, "Yes, I have heard it all."

"And what do you say about all this, my love?" I asked her. She looked radiant.

"My Emperor," she replied with a lilting bow, "I have but one thing to say."

Then she withdrew the golden blade and placed it at my feet, speaking in a voice so all could hear, "I Hail thee, Jon Kirk, Emperor of the Green Empire, Emperor of Ares, and now Emperor of the Known Universe!"

I sighed, well that did it, Sirah had just closed the deal. There was no way I could go against her wishes and not accept their honor now.

Suddenly the room broke out in thunderous cheers and wild applause. I nodded to them all, smiled, then walked over to hug my beloved Sirah. She held me tightly, then whispered into my ear softly, "I do hate to share you, my husband. First with Ares, and now it appears I must share you with all the Known Universe, but I do so proudly. You will make a great Emperor. We need you. They need you!"

I kissed her firmly on the mouth and more cheers rang throughout the chamber.

Zaor came forward, chanted out loudly, "All Hail, Jon Kirk, Emperor!

The chant was repeated three times by every voice in that chamber, then repeated many times more. It seemed like it would never end. The crowd showed their delight and I was truly touched by their warm feelings towards me. I knew I would do all I could and work hard to earn their respect and honor, and the faith they had placed in me here today.

My ears rang with the cheering, I hugged Sirah tightly and asked her with a sly grin, "Now what am I going to do?"

Sirah just told me, "We will think of that when the time comes."

I nodded, that was true, not everything had to be done at once, right away. I stood tall and accepted the cheers and good wishes of the enthusiastic crowd. All my friends and representatives of other cities, and other worlds, were there and gave me their good wishes. It was a heady mixture. The cheers and good words went on for a long time and it became a most joyous occasion. The excitement was electric and I could not help but become caught up in the joy and good feelings as I spoke and joked with old friends and new.

I did not notice the shimmering area suddenly growing in the center of the room until I could see an image forming there.

CHAPTER 16

LORD DOOM'S RETURN

The light grew and glowed and now everyone in the huge chamber was noticing it too. Suddenly fear and panic was growing around us like a living thing. What could it be? Now an image was seen to be formed there, and there was a gasp of terror from the crowd, for many of us recognized that vile image quite well. Sirah and I most of all.

It was the Sindalki traitor and murderer, Lord Karlath Doom!

I starred at him for a second in disbelief, transfixed as he just materialized there right before my eyes. The crowd saw him too and could not believe it. Was it really him, or just some spectral image? Some ghost? Then I got over my shock and my attention focused the important matters at hand and what this might mean. Were we under attack? Was the rest of the enemy fleet here now? Had the enemy attack already begun?

I looked toward Quarto with my questions, but he told me firmly there was no danger yet, there was no attack as far as he could tell. No enemy space fleet was in the area. So what now?

It was Aron of Keva who explained, "Doom has come for you, Jon Kirk. I am able to repulse some of his power, but he can repulse some of my own as well. We are at an impasse regarding the higher powers here. So we are left with the merely physical powers you each possess. You must fight him on your own, and you must defeat him!"

I drew my sword, ready for whatever might come.

I cried out, "Doom, you have boldness coming here! Is it truly you, or some ghostly image? Where is your fleet, your ships, your master Kin-Ty-Roo?"

"I need no master nor ships to destroy you, Jon Kirk! I am here now to battle you in the flesh, man to man!" Doom growled as he now drew a long jeweled sword. I looked at him closely, if he really was here in person, this was a chance in a lifetime for me to take him down. I would take him now!

Doom snarled looking over at Aron, "That one over there has great powers I had not anticipated, he can block my own powers quite well, so I can not use beams, rays or living fire this time upon you. So that is as it may be. Instead I will be more than happy to use my sword, which can not be blocked or interfered with on this physical plane, and I will use it to cut you into pieces!"

"Then come and get me!" I barked, but instead of waiting for him to attack I ran towards Doom with my blade out and ready. I struck at him hard, our blades clanging loudly. There was definitely substance behind the form. That shook me. Was this actually the physical body of Lord Doom? Was he really here in person, as he had said? There was a gasp from everyone in the chamber, a mob and crowd that quickly moved to create a large circle around us to view the deadly epic battle.

Doom was real—and he was quick and a surprisingly good swordsman. I was surprised and did not realize that Sindalki culture placed such a high regard upon good swordsmanship. However, I still had my ace in the hole when it came to any battle, for my Earthly muscles gave me incredible power and stamina. So I knew I was more than an equal for Doom in any fair fight, but I also knew that this would probably *not* be a fair fight.

Now my adversary came at me hard, guttural grunts of animal rage were heard as his sword struck my own many times. We crashed blades back and forth, each looking for an opening. I blocked his blade each time, but he also blocked mine.

"It will be a pleasure to spill your guts, Jon Kirk!"

"Or, I your own!" I replied forcefully.

Doom just growled and tried to strike me a glancing blow on the left shoulder. I backed off before it landed, regrouped, then came back at him. My attack was stronger this time and caused him to move off, then he lost his balance and I saw a chance to move in on him. I twisted my blade and slipped it past his guard to nick his arm. I was rewarded by seeing a thin trickle of red blood run down his arm.

"So you do bleed!" I cried in the full heat of battle rage. Seeing that blood made me come at him all the harder. Now I saw that he could be killed, I knew I really could win this fight. It was possible! That was all I needed to know.

Lord Doom laughed, "You think you can kill me? You have no idea of the forces I have at my command should I desire to use them. But I do not want to use them on you, Jon Kirk, what I want is to gut you like the animal you are! I want to personally cut you into tiny pieces right here in front of all your people! And I will!"

"Shut up and fight!" I barked, his words were annoying me, and making me nervous. I slashed with my sword, just missing his head, he regrouped and came at me with a rapid attack that pushed me back and then he thrust at my chest. Somehow I twisted out of the way of his blade, then came around and gave him a sword thrust of my own.

It was a tie as to which one of us was more shocked by what happened next.

My blade struck, it went towards his chest and cut him. No one was more shocked that my gambit had worked than I. Doom looked at me in utter surprise as well, he tried to get his sword up at me as he swung his body away. I stood firm, knocking away his blade as I dug my own blade into him deeper. He screamed, I plunged my blade into his chest ever deeper, into his very heart—if the fiend had one—blood began to spurt. I knew I had him now.

My blade drove into him deep, all his resistance to me now suddenly stopped, as he looked at me in uncomprehending surprise. Then he gasped in pain, shuttered and quickly died. I withdrew my blade from his chest, shaking my head in disbelief, shock, surprise. I was shaking myself now. Was he really dead? It was almost too much to believe. Too much to hope for.

Lord Doom lay upon the floor of my palace audience chamber in the center of a large circle formed by a thousand frenzied onlookers—all of whom had been cheering me on—and now cheered for me ever louder. They looked upon Doom with contempt and hatred—but also terrible fear. I could not fault them for their feelings, yet all feared to approach too close to the body, like it was some unclean thing that might bite them.

I walked over and carefully checked Doom's body. His wound was deep and extensive, dark red blood was pooling on the floor at my feet. There was no pulse. That was that. Lord Doom was most definitely dead. I gave a deep sigh of relief, looking upon the body but hearing all the cheers lauding my epic victory. Maybe now that Doom was dead, Sirah and my son would now be safe. I prayed that it would be so.

"He is dead! That is the end of him!" I shouted to all in victory and obvious relief.

More cheers rang up from the crowd.

"Doom is dead!" they chanted in growing voices.

"Lord Doom is dead!" they chanted enthusiastically.

Aron came forward, "You have done well, Jon Kirk, My Emperor."

I wiped my sweaty face, then smiled, "Thank you."

"No, thank you. Now Shamar and I will leave, but first we will take Lord Kneth with us. We of Kev may be able to help him."

I looked towards Admiral Quarto about this request, and he nodded in agreement.

"Yes, then take him with you and heal him as best you can," I said.

"We shall do the best that is possible," Aron told me simply.

"Well, then thank you for your words of wisdom and your friendship."

"It is Shamar and I who thank you, Jon Kirk, Our Emperor."

I nodded, yes, I was Emperor now, so be it, I offered them a wry grin.

Then Shamar and Aron took Lord Kneth between them and suddenly they were gone. All three just disappeared. It was magical, mystical, amazing. The crowd cheered and began talking wildly about their magnificent powers. There was a lot of joyous feelings just then. Thank the gods the Kevans were on our side for they had great powers, but so did our enemies I remembered.

I was thinking about that fact when I looked over at the dead body of Lord Doom where it still lay upon the bloody floor. It had not been taken away yet. He had been a dangerous monster that would bother us no longer. I sighed with relief that he was dead and gone. He was one more enemy I did not have to worry about any longer.

It was then that I saw his finger move.

My gaze did an immediate double-take as a cold feeling of dread grabbed hold of me. Cold sweat ran down my back. I suddenly heard mumblings around me within the chamber, the crowd was moving backwards from the corpse, there were whispers and then cries of fear.

I heard someone scream, "He is coming back to life!"

I shuddered. That could not be! However as I looked hard at Lord Doom I noticed there was movement in his fingers and hands. His leg twitched. What was happening?

I drew my sword and stood over the body, watching and waiting.

Then Doom's body just as suddenly went limp and remained totally motionless. Everyone was shocked, starring in fear, I felt cold sweat run down my neck. There was no more movement for a long moment. I watched and waited to make sure. That seemed the end of it. Soon we were all relieved.

I realized that what we had seen must have been a death rattle, or some kind of delayed release of the spirit into the Afterworld. I could not figure it. No one there could. We all stood looking down at the body of Doom amazed by what we had seen, fearful the monster was not dead, but now relieved that it evidently must be truly dead. It had to be.

Then Lord Karlath Doom suddenly stood up upon his feet in one rapid movement as if waking up from a long sleep. He quickly stood tall and straight before us. He was no longer bleeding. He was no longer injured. He quickly picked up his bejeweled sword and replaced it into his scabbard. There was an evil smirk of victory upon his face.

Chaos reigned around him. Most people just looked on frozen in utter astonishment, the monster had come back to life - if in fact he had ever truly been alive to begin with —or killed at all. For now he was certainly not dead! He had somehow reanimated himself!

Some people panicked and ran out of the chamber screaming in terror.

My eyes locked upon the eyes of the living monster with determination and terror.

"I find the most surprising thing about dying—is returning to life!" Lord Doom shouted loudly with positive glee. He appeared to be in no pain at all. He had no injury. He looked at us all with wild arrogance. "You should all see the looks upon your faces!"

I gripped my sword tightly and charged at him in a deadly rage. If he did not die before when I had killed him, then I would make sure he died now. Then I would cut him up into so many pieces he would never be able to regenerate.

"Die Doom!" I cried as I charged him with my blade to strike him down.

Doom just sneered at me as he was quickly surrounded by a shimmering light, "You have failed, Jon Kirk!"

Then he was gone.

He just disappeared!

"Doom! Come back here! You coward!"

I screamed at him in impotent rage as all around me became utter chaos.

Zaor finally came over to me and put his hand upon my shoulder in brotherly affection, "He is gone, Jon Kirk. Let it be. One battle is over, let us now look to the one that is coming."

I nodded, Zaor was right, so I held down my frustration and anger. I told him, "We will be ready, my friend. Next time, we will be the ones who bring defeat to our enemies."

Sirah then came over to me and we embraced as one. It was then that I remembered what was truly important in life. I still had my wife and son safe, I still had my world of Ares safe. With all that, anything is possible.

I still live!

EPILOG

We were back again on the Earth now. In my living room. I sat spell-bound across from my good friend Jon Kirk, in the most comfortable room of my house as he finished his narrative.

"Surely Lord Doom has some other plan of revenge? What was it? And is Earth safe? Are we safe here from him?" I anxiously asked.

"No, I am afraid nothing is safe now, but he and his master most certainly have a plan, and I can tell you it was a terrible plan worthy of such monsters—and it almost worked."

"So you—so it has already happened? So you were victorious because you are here now."

"Yes and no, it is hard to describe the space-time facts of this future tale, but all that is a story for another night, my friend."

I sighed, "And this Enemy Empire and this self-styled Emperor of The Known Universe…? I mean, not you…but…him…it?"

Jon Kirk laughed warmly, "Yes, they forced that title upon me, but it is just a title, just words as Aron The Eldest told me. But, yes, that was most interesting. I think you will like that story also, when next I tell it to you."

I smiled at him, amazed and champing at the bit for more, but I did not want to press my friend too hard as I could see that it was getting late and talking about this part of his story seemed to cause him some obvious distress. I wondered why?

"Well, I can see it is getting late here, my old friend, and I must be getting back. Old Tar-gool's machinery is unreliable at best, one reason why it took me so long to visit you again—and I must leave here and get back to Sirah. I also have a trip that I soon must take to the mysterious city of Kev, for Lord Kneth awaits."

"I see. Well I hope your next visit here will not be so long in coming."

Jon Kirk just smiled and told me, "We'll see, my friend, we'll see. Until the next time."

Then the transmission ended and the image of Jon Kirk faded away to vanish in the air before me like he had never been there at all. In fact, Jon Kirk had not actually been there at all, merely his image, his voice, and his narrative—that story of his life and adventures upon the faraway planet Ares.

But what a story!

I knew that I would have to wait patiently for the next installment of Jon Kirk's wild adventures and I wondered what life had in store for him, his beloved Sirah, their little son, Alun, and the wondrous planet Ares—and now, the planets of all the Known Universe! I was sure that it would prove another strange tale well worth waiting for!

ABOUT THE AUTHOR

GARY LOVISI is a Brooklyn-based author and science fiction fan who was inspired early in life by the John Carter of Mars books—and all the great works of Edgar Rice Burroughs—which he first read as a teenager in the 1960s. In his Jon Kirk of Ares Chronicles, he seeks to capture the sense of wonder, rousing pulsepounding action, and strange adventures on alien worlds, that made Burroughs' classic books so much fun to read. Lovisi has written in all genres of fiction, from short stories to novels; and non-fiction about authors, artists, and book collecting. He edits Paperback Parade magazine and founded Gryphon Books. He was short-listed for a Mystery Writers of America Edgar Award for the Best Short Story of the Year, and received a Spur Award from the Western Writers of America. Lovisi's first Jon Kirk of Ares novel, *The Winged-Men* was published by Wildside Press in 2014. Now with these two latest original novels in the series from Wildside Press: *The Invisible Men* (#2) and *The Space Men* (#3), the Jon Kirk of Ares Chronicles is off and running, with more original novels planned. To find out more about Lovisi, his writing, other books, or Jon Kirk of Ares Chronicles news, check his website: www.gryphonbooks.com.

ABOUT THE COVER ARTIST

MARCUS BOAS is a New York City illustrator, and a master of vivid fantasy and science fiction art. His use of striking colors and heroic images in his art dazzles all who view it. His stunning work has been a mainstay used on the covers of many books and magazines in the fantasy field over his decades long art career. A big fan of Edgar Rice Burroughs, and especially the John Carter of Mars series, Marcus is a natural to do the covers for the Jon Kirk of Ares Chronicles. You can see some of his outstanding work collected in such books as *Heroic Fantasy, Jungle*, and others published by Kaso Comics at www.kasocomics.com. Wonderful prints are also available for some of his most beautiful work.

ABOUT THE MAPMAKER

LUCILLE CALI is a Brooklyn, New York free-lance artist whose map of Ares is based upon the original map first drawn by the author in 1971, when he wrote the first book in the Jon Kirk of Ares Chronicles. Cali has done numerous covers for various Gryphon Books as well as issues of *Hardboiled* magazine and is a very versatile artist.

www.ingramcontent.com/pod-product-compliance
Lightning Source LLC
Chambersburg PA
CBHW020142180626
46810CB00004B/1695